IN THE SPARROW HILLS

IN THE SPARROW HILLS

Stories by

Emile Capouya

Algonquin Books of
Chapel Hill
1993

This is a work of fiction. While, as in all fiction, the literary perceptions and insights are based on experience, all names, characters, places, and incidents are either products of the author's imagination or are used fictitiously. No reference to any real person is intended or should be inferred.

Published by
ALGONQUIN BOOKS OF CHAPEL HILL
Post Office Box 2225
Chapel Hill, North Carolina 27515-2225
a division of WORKMAN
PUBLISHING COMPANY, INC.
708 Broadway
New York, New York 10003

Design by Barbara E. Williams.
Printed in the United States of America.

LIBRARY OF CONGRESS CATALOGING-IN-PUBLICATION DATA
Capouya, Emile.
In the Sparrow Hills :
stories by Emile Capouya.
p cm.
ISBN 0-945575-62-9
I. Title.
PS3553.A5885S7 1993
813′.54—dc20 92-31780 CIP

2 4 6 8 10 9 7 5 3 1
First Edition

To the memory
of my father.

CONTENTS

ACKNOWLEDGMENTS

THE following stories first appeared in *The Antioch Review:*
"In the Sparrow Hills,"
"A Dream of Fair Women,"
"The Other Rogozhin," and
"A Parenthesis."

IN THE SPARROW HILLS

IN THE SPARROW HILLS

THIS IS NOT a story. The people I mention here for purposes of corroboration are men of flesh and blood—or, as the Spaniards say, more tellingly, men of flesh and bone. Two of them are very much alive, and the third not long dead, all of them public figures in a small way, the only way in which literary men in our time are likely to be public figures if there is anything to them. I have no hesitation about mentioning their names. I haven't asked their permission, but the matter in regard to which I want them to back me with their testimony is a question of fact, quite impersonal. The one who is no longer alive can scarcely be my witness in any active sense, and yet he is for my purposes the most important of the three, since the business I have in mind falls directly within his professional specialty. I hope to be believed when I report what he said about it because I met him when I was very young, he was kind to me for something like thirty years, and I took the liberty of loving him. That is, I hope to be believed because it should be clear that I would not invoke his spirit falsely. Besides, we human beings live by trust. In this city, if you ask a passerby for directions the chances are very good that he will misdirect you. But I should judge that the chances of being purposely misdirected are just about zero. People are always in a hurry here. People are always confused. Only when they are abstracted does the look of confusion leave their faces—and then, when you awaken a stranger from his dream and put to him a puzzle in geography, about a place where he himself finds his way without reflection, by habit, it is only to be expected that his hurried answer will not always meet an ideal standard of accuracy.

I was thinking about all that the other evening in the restaurant. Then the waitress brought the bill, I looked at it, I handed her a credit card, and I went back to thinking about the propriety of mentioning Avrahm Yarmolinsky in order to have the support of his name for what I mean to say. I was thinking that the mere suspicion that I might be citing him for interested motives after his death would in a sense slander him by associating him with those interested motives. And I was thinking that since my motives were reducible to one, to establish a point of literary history on his testimony and that of two other gentlemen, I didn't see why anyone would want to impugn my credit. It's as if I were to announce that I had broken my leg in early March of 1965, as in fact I did do, and people who knew me at the time know that I did, though they cannot be expected to recollect the month and the year. Now, if I were to make that statement, why should it awaken doubts, and reflect badly on the integrity of my witnesses? The waitress came back and said, "Sorry, sir, your card has been declined."

She is a brusque, rawboned young woman. Not many weeks ago I was in the restaurant, and her hoarse voice sounded suddenly from the kitchen: "When I heard the Pope was dead I just freaked out. I mean I just freaked out." There was no mistaking the excitement in her tone, but since I couldn't see her face I had no way of judging the quality of her excitement. What sounded like a note of jubilation was almost certainly something else. It was hard to imagine that her life was so empty of excitement that she welcomed the Pope's death because it relieved the tedium. I call the place a restaurant, but it's more gin mill than restaurant, much more gin mill. It's just down the block and in that sense convenient, but it's noisy at night, lots of action, and waitressing is hard work. No doubt there's plenty of tedium in it, but plenty of excitement too. It wouldn't be that. But her words told me nothing by themselves—the beauty of that language is that it doesn't give anything away—and I could not see her face. I remember that I felt more friendly to her because she had been stirred, in some way, by the death of that old man.

She had slapped the card upon the table, as a cardplayer slaps down a card in triumph or disgust, and had turned away about her other business before I had understood what she had said. Declined? The term was oddly decorous. Had I gone beyond my limit? It was possible. When cash is short you use the card to take up the slack, and then card on card. But I was sure that I had paid the last installment. Or even if I hadn't, the credit company would not yet have had time to publish my card number with those of other delinquents in the closely printed booklet. Did the restaurant have a direct line to the company, and had they telephoned? How strange. The likeliest thing was that someone had made a mistake. And I began to feel offended that a regular customer should be treated so offhandedly when there was a good chance that he was not at fault. Then I noticed that the bill, too, was back on the table. I took out a ten and two singles, put them on top of the bill, and set about finishing my beer.

The waitress sailed by and picked up the money, awkward but swift. As she did, I saw something out of place, and a moment later I knew what it was. I had seen two tens and a single rise from the table with the bill. But if I was right about that, then I had made a mistake earlier when I thought I had taken a ten and two singles from my wallet. I counted the money I had left. It seemed about ten dollars short. But I am not reliable when it comes to things of that kind. I finished my beer, thinking that if I had overpaid the waitress, she'd soon be back.

She didn't come. The man behind the bar saw me tilt my

chair and look round for her. He asked if he could help me. I told him my credit card had been refused, I didn't know why, but in any case I had given the waitress cash, a ten and two singles, I had thought, and then I had had the impression that it was a single and two tens. He said she'd be back. After a moment she appeared. "The check was $10.09. I gave the bartender a ten and nine cents and kept the two singles for my tip. Here, this is what I have in my pocket." She showed me a roll of singles. "I don't have a ten on me." I said, "Oh, I'm sorry. That's fine, then." And I felt relieved. I got up and went out into the street. But while walking I saw two tens and a single rise from the table, and I remembered that I seemed to be ten dollars short. But why would she have done a thing like that? I wasn't drunk. I had had a bottle of beer with my dinner. It would have been foolish of her to do a thing like that deliberately. At worst she had made a mistake, just as I certainly had done. To suspect her would be unjust. Besides, it was simply too painful to suspect people. We live by trust.

Now, I want to offer Avrahm Yarmolinsky's testimony on one small point—and certainly not least because I feel honored to be able to mention his name as that of a friend. Of course, he was a great scholar, and everyone respects such attainments. But, on the other hand, only a scholar in Yarmolinsky's field could really appreciate him on that ground. For me, respect for his learning was partly a form of superstition, relying on evidence of things unseen, the vulgar kind of faith that has the effect of making certain people popular because they are popular. What really moved me was his character.

For many years he was head of the Slavic Languages Division of the New York Public Library, and he worked at the Forty-second Street building. Whenever I enter that mausoleum I feel entombed. But though he spoke gently and was naturally self-effacing, as befitted a senior servitor of that great mortuary of books, he showed how much spirit and passion could find lodgment in such a place. His figure was slight, so that he looked like a grown-up boy, and he had a diffidence that seemed adolescent. His silences seemed adolescent, but if they arose out of shyness I never felt that they were self-regarding. In his presence my own tormenting social awkwardness lost much of its burden of self-regard. When I used to visit him and he would come forward to shake my hand—carrying his own hands in an odd way, knuckles to the fore—his Russian head that was shaped like a slender keystone, with the short, stiff hair brushed up *al Umberto*, would be slightly tilted and would be regarding me like a block of cordial granite. After our hands had met, his eyes would shift gratefully elsewhere, and the ceremony of greeting, made difficult by affection, would have been successfully accomplished.

He had very little small talk and no grand pronouncements. I have never known a man who inquired how you were with so clear an intention of listening to the answer. It used to make me feel as if I were talking to my father, and must be careful not to hurt him by giving too blunt an account of my life and prospects. On the other hand I felt obliged to tell him the truth, and I managed it by telling him generalities: I found my job difficult because publishing houses were likely to be ignorant or venal—things of that sort. I knew that if I were to give him instances or details I should soon grow passionate and afflict him with my professional *déboires.* That is what usually happened when I talked about those things with my own father, for he used to question me with an affectionate pertinacity born of his illusion that his son was a romantic who needed to be protected from the impulse to footless martyrdom. But he himself was the romantic idealist, as his brothers often told him, and not by way of praise. He had managed to live decently, honorably, in a world now quite vanished. I had earned my living in the new world by compounding with the enemy on every important point. My father imagined that I was baring my breast to all God's dangers, like the heroic Swiss who gathered the spears of six spearmen into his bosom to make a breach in the enemy rank through which his comrades might pass. So when my father, affectionately reproachful, and with mild irony for what he supposed was my moonstruck vision of the world of commerce, would press me for the story of my latest discomfiture, I would lose all self-control, and tell him the circumstances of the prehistory of the incident, and then its history, and at last I would impart to him my moral reflections upon it—sometimes an hour's business. At the end of it he would be shaking his head sadly, and I would feel that I had abused him, for he is candid as a child and the news of the world's small evils appalls him forever. On one of those occasions he said to me, "What I cannot understand is that you haven't sat down with your boss and explained those things to him. He would surely see that it must be in everyone's interest to abandon such a policy—if policy it can be called, since it is so clearly retrograde." And after that demonstration of his hopeless good faith and naïveté I felt especially tender to him. He was a spar from the wreck of that old world, adrift in the new, unconscious that when the skies change, men's hearts change with the skies.

Avrahm Yarmolinsky was innocent in the same way, but he never pressed me. He may have been too diffident to examine his own sons and prescribe for them. In any case our relations did not authorize anything of the kind. It was I who asked most of the questions, and these were generally of the impersonal sort. I would ask him about Russian and Soviet literature—like most Americans I have almost no acquaintance with the literatures of the other Slavs. I remember him saying, with a pained smile, something like, "The literature of the recent Soviet period is really quite poor. Pasternak, Solzhenitsyn—those immensely gifted writers are not at all characteristic. They have skipped over generations, going back for their inspiration to the great Russian masters of the nineteenth century. A novelist like Sholokhov is a vigorous writer—one of few—but he has nothing like the imagination of the great nineteenth-century writers, nothing like their psychological penetration, let alone their moral impetus and philosophic power." All this hesitantly, with a pained smile from first to last.

Yet I had seen him an energumen. When I was in my early twenties, it must have been shortly after the war, I was his guest at a dinner party. Among the other guests was an affable man with a guitar—I gathered he was a neighbor—who sang very pleasantly, "The fox he run to his cozy den, there were his little ones, eight, nine, ten . . ." And there was a young Czech woman, large limbed and handsome, who took the guitar from him and sang something softly, her voice low and moving. There were two Poles, I think, and a Yugoslav. At times when no one sang, Yarmolinsky talked to his Slavic friends with startling volubility, turning from one to the other, and shifting from one tongue to another as if he were a mere mindless polyglot—but speaking in so emphatic a tone and with such evident high spirits that he seemed transformed by enthusiasm. It may be that while he wrote English very well, he did not really feel at home in the language, so that it was a relief to his spirit to talk with animated Slavs.

I never afterwards saw him exhibit anything approaching abandon, but I had been pleased by that evidence of fire as a youngster is apt to be pleased, and liked him the more for it.

It was the memory of having seen him exhilarated in that way that persuaded me to tell him, many years later, of a literary admiration of mine. I don't know why I am so disinclined to speak of such things ordinarily, but I am. Mostly, I am ashamed to speak of them. Among persons of a certain social class, as I have noticed, or at least in certain circles, enthusiasms of the kind are common coin. And I have worked in a trade—the book trade—in which grown men often say, "That's a manuscript that I'm really excited about." Perhaps it's because they say it often that my stomach turns. Perhaps it's because the expression, in a man's mouth, sounds faintly androgynous. But chiefly I think it is a kind of shrinking snobbery on my part that makes me take their professional excitement so seriously, since I know very well that they are not exposing their intimate feelings when they say things of the sort. Their emotion is aroused by the qualities that the manuscript in question offers under the aspect of a commodity. Everyone in the trade understands that very well. And in what sense would it be useful for people in a publishing house to be susceptible to the appeal of a manuscript that was destined to fall stone dead in the market? My snobbery isn't a response to the vulgarity of an enthusiasm domesticated for the purpose of selling books. It's that I shrink from avowing any literary enthusiasm at all, as if the subject were unfit for mention in mixed company. And the ebullient interest that the trade takes in books on which one can make a decent profit, for all its seeming innocence, its genuine innocence, glances too nearly at this foible of mine, simply because the object of the emotion is something that has been written. I am far from being immune to the values expressed in the practice of publishing houses; if you were, you couldn't work in one. No, I share them fully. But I feel it isn't decent to proclaim those values because in the nature of things they are at least distantly related to the ones that arise from genuine works of literature. That is an odd scruple that I myself cannot account for—seeing that I have spent many years in the trade—and that I am not at all proud of. If I were to be honest I should have to say that my violent delicacy on this question is cousin to my abhorrence of the waitress's patchouli. For she moves in a nimbus of the scent. She leaves it on the edge of a dish, on the lip of a glass, on the silver. Sometimes I am assailed by the smell hours later if I pass my hand near to my face. When that happens I can't understand how it is that I never remember how much I dislike the smell of the waitress until I have actually crossed the threshold of that restaurant. And certainly I know that a hoarse voice and patchouli do not amount to moral obliquity. She is a young woman, doing the things that are socially available for her to do. At most her pungent musk represents a social error, and not even that, no doubt, among her friends, who must include people who are estimable by any reasonable standard and yet are in no way affronted by the use of strong perfumes. I cannot bear it, pe I am not such a fool as to make the practice my decency, honor, self-respect.

The fact is that there is an ugly streak in my character, a kind of repercussive violence that I am well aware of and should be happy to be without. When I was young it sometimes took dangerous forms. The war had been over for a couple of months when I sailed as AB on the *Waterbury Victory*, New York to Antwerp, in midwinter. I was the only AB on the ship who had a ticket—the others were acting ABs and by law could go no higher than ten feet above the deck. The first day out, the mate had me go aloft to the mainmast truck to chip and paint my way down the mast. I eased into a bosun's chair, with a chipping hammer, a wire brush, and a pot of red lead secured to the chair's bridle, and a marlinspike on a rope-yarn lanyard over one shoulder and across my breast. It was blowing half a gale, and I was swayed aloft by my gantline, whose end had been taken to the winch. The bosun tended my line, and he ran me up steadily, but he couldn't do anything to keep the roll of the vessel from knocking me about. The *Waterbury Victory* was a famous roller. Later on during that passage, to see just how she rolled, I rigged a clinometer in the crew's mess, a hacksaw blade pivoted on a nail in the bulkhead, and the degrees of its swing shown on an arc drawn with a protractor. The certificate on the bridge said that the ship was rated for forty degrees. The men took the clinometer down at last because she would roll to forty-four and hang there a long time before rolling as far the other way. On this day she gave me a pounding. I reached the truck with bruised knees and skinned knuckles, in a temper that they would think to send a man aloft to do an anytime job when it was blowing fresh.

When I was nearly at the truck I balled up a fist and thrust it out to one side for the bosun to see. At once he slacked the line on the windlass drum and held me motionless. Then I made to marry the two parts of my gantline to hold me in place while he threw the line off the windlass. But I saw that the dangling paint pot would foul the long bight of line that I must overhaul with my free hand, in order to bring it up through the bridle and up and over my body to make the hitch that would support me aloft and allow me to descend at will, a few inches at a time. So I put out my fist again, looking down sidelong towards the winch and calling to the bosun to hold it. He nodded. It took me a few moments to shorten the tail on the pot and secure it to the other leg of the bridle. As I turned from doing that, the chair fell eight feet.

It would have fallen farther, but I had had a hand on one part of the gantline, and I had married it to the other almost before I knew that I was falling. Now with both hands holding the lines together, I looked below me. The bosun was gone, and one of the ordinaries, a green boy, was at the winch. Or rather six feet away and with his back to it. I shouted at him, and he began to haul me up with a snap that broke my grasp on the gantline and burned my hands. I shouted again and he stopped. It took a long time to make him understand that he must throw the turns off the winch. One's strength goes quickly aloft. I was weak by the time I started to haul up the long bight of the gantline with my right hand. There were many pauses, when I took the strain by pressing the line against the chair's bridle with my thigh, and it was a painful business getting a long loop through the bridle, and my legs and then the whole rig through the loop, till the hitch was formed at the bridle's throat. Then I sat for a while, getting over my scare and waiting for the strength to come back to my arms. I was safe now, and under my own steam, and the thing to do would be to stand on the seat of the bosun's chair, one hand for the ship and one hand for myself, and start to chip away at that six foot of topmast that I could no longer reach while sitting. But after a while it was clear that I hadn't the strength to wriggle my knees up above the level of the seat and pull myself to a standing position. By now, too, I had passed a frapping line around the mast to keep me from surging as the ship rolled, for her course kept us nearly in the trough of the sea; I was afraid to cast off that line and try to stand up. So I began to work where I was. My arms were so nearly numb that I had to shift the hammer from hand to hand.

Then the bosun called me from below. He motioned furiously, telling me to go higher. I shook my head. I attacked the mast again. A little after that I heard him shout from much closer. He had run up the ladder, which went as high as the crosstrees, and some twenty-five feet below me he was bellowing in the wind. He was tall and powerfully made, black Irish with raging blue eyes. The wind was so high that it stirred the thick black mustache bowed over the mouth that was venting fury at my bad seamanship. It seemed to me that I could see down his throat. I had been shivering in my thin clothes, mostly from weakness, but in an instant that was over. Seizing the heavy marlinspike that hung from my shoulder, I broke the lanyard with a jerk. "Boats, you left a green kid to tend my gantline. I'll settle with you when we're both on deck. Now stand from under or I'll drop this spike point-first." The bosun was a thorough seaman. His expression showed that he was appalled, not by the threat but by the breach of discipline—I must be raving mad. Almost at once he lowered his head and began to descend the ladder. He must have been a bold man, too, because he never looked up to see what I might be at.

I had painted my way down to the crosstrees when I was called for my wheel watch. The paint locker was housed in the mast tabernacle on deck, and I stowed my painting gear there and drew kerosene from a drum with a spigot on it to clean up a bit before going to the wheel. I was in a fever, but I did not see the bosun. On the bridge the man at the wheel told me the course and that she was carrying a little left rudder as she sheered away from the seas. I saw nothing in his expression, nor in the mate's. But I was in no condition to notice, and from the bridge the mate, at least, may have seen something amazing, a sailor aloft holding out a marlinspike over the bosun's head. When my watch was over, I saw the bosun in the mess, but we did not speak. The next day during my watch I went to the paint locker, and the bosun, his back to me, was mixing paint. He sang,

How can it be, you fair young maiden,
No man has taken you to wife?
Are all the lads or blind or crazy?
Or do you love your single life?

I stopped a few feet from him. He stirred paint and sang. After a while I moved forward again, and he turned and handed me the paint pot, saying, "There you are." And that was that. Except that I reflected for the first time that I had offered to kill a man because he had been somewhat overbearing. I thought, too, that my father, with his soldierly sense of duty, would feel consternation if he were to hear of it. But since then I have done other foolish things.

Now, I mean to make a small point of literary history, not compose a work of art. If I were telling a story, I would do it according to the rules. I would not ruminate on things widely separated, and I would not be the subject of my own reflections. The work would be a narrative, it would have a shape, it would be faithful to itself. But I am engaged in something of a very different order, in which I am forced to speak of myself, and these wandering reflections are a way I have found that will permit me to talk about something that must seem surprising. These scattered memories as they arise have the effect of inspiriting me to go on to the historical matter I have it at heart to deliver. They remind me that I have a life, a self, as real as other men's — something I lose sight of whenever I am called to say what is counter to received opinion, or is simply unexpected, and if only for that reason somewhat disobliging. Then I doubt my right to speak. The sensation is of an attack of moral dizziness. But I should like to be able to persuade the reader, not that presently he will learn something to his advantage, as the writers of mystery stories used to say, but that he will learn something unexpected. Each new thing, it seems to me, changes the shape of the world. So I trust that all this military music, artless in the worst sense, will not prove a mere imposition when I have come to saying what it has been given to me to say.

I told Avrahm Yarmolinsky about a story of Chekhov that I had read while I was in college. It was in a volume that had the look of penury about it, bound in a cheap gray cloth filled with an unpleasant sizing, and the reedy lettering stamped in a blue that must always have looked faded and pinched. But that Chekhov collection had been assigned in a course I was taking, and I was glad to have come upon the last copy in the library. I was at college soon after the war. Many of the men in my class had been in the service for a long time; it was a great luxury for them to be in a college and reading books. They were eager to read, so that the books reserved for particular courses were hard to find. I carried off my dispirited-looking prize with satisfaction, and the two moods attended me as I read the stories. All of them appeared to me to have been composed expressly to be gathered into a volume bound in shoddy gray cloth with watery stamping. Nevertheless, to my astonishment, they were desolating and exalting.

One of those stories has been with me ever since. A gentleman walks out into the country—was it on the outskirts of St. Petersburg or of Moscow? The latter, perhaps, for I think I remember mention of the Sparrow Hills. Winter is near. The day is somber. Wandering absently, the gentleman is only half aware of the signs of the dying year about him, but his musings have taken their tone from the brown landscape and the wintry light. Then he comes upon a shepherd. Greeting him, he remarks on the cheerless look that the day has taken on. And after a moment the shepherd makes him this answer: "Your honor, the world is running down. A few years ago in these parts you would start a hare from his form at every step. If you paused among the poplars, the grouse would startle you with the sudden noise of his wings—sometimes two, three, four in succession bursting from the copse, each one taking you by surprise. The geese have been flying south all this month, but they are few, and most go by in silence. All my life long I was used to hear them before they could be seen, calling with a sound like the barking of dogs far off, and the flocks were so great that the long double line stretched to the limit of sight. The ducks are few now, too, in this season when they should be many. And each year in spring the woodcock would call in the clearings at twilight, then fly into the air and circle high up, and plummet down with their wild whistle—times I have heard them three at once, calling and whistling in different places. None came this past spring. The ewes scarcely bear. The grass is thin. The health is gone out of the world.

"Men are sickly in body and spirit. For how could the increase fail and man's life be sound?"

And at these words the gentleman's heart contracts as if for a long time he has been suffering unaware and has just heard the name of his trouble. Or as if he has long been suppressing a painful intuition, and now his fellow has given it expression in terms that sweep away his resistance and leave him unmanned.

Something like that happened to me in New Orleans long ago, during the war. I was ashore, waiting for a ship, and so as not to be idle I had taken a job breaking freight for a trucking company. I worked at night, loading drums of lard, barrels of flour, cases and cartons of general merchandise for Shreveport or Lafayette or as far as Birmingham. It was interesting work. Sometimes the boss would give me directions, but mostly the strategy of loading was left to me, and I found it like ship stowage, though a good deal more simple since the tractor-trailer was not expected to roll and pitch with the seas. But still there was the job of getting the mass of goods out of the shed and into the trailer in the best order and with a minimum of double handling. It was tactically interesting, too. To break back a drum that weighed more than I did, slide the tongue of the handtruck under it, draw it onto the handtruck, and start the load moving forward in the same instant in order to gain enough momentum on the narrow dock to be able to run it up the steel ramp into the body of the trailer—that took a little doing. And the heavy things had to be placed to best advantage, the case goods and cartons had to be stacked in bulkheads so that they would not shift. The time went quickly between ten-thirty at night and four-thirty in the morning, and when I needed to straighten my back it was lawful to light a cigarette. Since it was summer, I would be going home in the first light. It was good work.

I was thinking of all that and feeling pleased as I knocked off one morning. I had just been paid. I had worked hard, but I had not been bored and I was not tired. I was looking forward to joining a ship in four days' time. I caught the streetcar. At the next stop a large blond man in white overalls boarded the car.

Though it was nearly empty, he took the seat beside me. He was in good spirits and he wanted to talk. He and his wife had come from Mississippi a few weeks ago so that he could take a job with a contractor who was building a government depot on the outskirts of the city. He said he did anything that had to do with framing—rough general carpentry for construction, as he summed it up. He added after a moment, "The money is good. And it's good work." That chimed in so well with my mood that when he asked me what I did I began to describe the pleasures of breaking freight. He said thoughtfully, "Every trade is interesting when you come to learn of it. Every trade." But I was anxious that he not think I was a warehouse laborer. I told him I was a seaman, and I began to talk of my art and mystery.

We had been sitting companionably in the rattling car, looking straight ahead but glancing at each other occasionally—it was a pleasure to look at his broad red open face, his fine mild eyes. But now he turned to me in surprise and commiseration. "Oh, you poor young man. Then you spend your life upon the sea. You have no woman to share your thoughts—" He broke off as if the idea were too immense for speech, or as if he felt that he had been indelicate in alluding to my friendless state. But after a while he said, "There's pain in every life. Now, this job of mine is a godsend for the money it pays. The crew are all decent fellows. But I have to work nights, you see. If only I could work days, why, I'd be happy as a bird." I asked him if there was no chance of changing to the day shift. He shook his head. "Seems not. I've asked." I had put the question in sympathy, of course, and out of politeness, but also to give myself a breathing space. I had to take account of a new idea that threatened to change the aspect of the world. I can scarcely recall now the sense of privilege I used to feel in bearing the discipline of the vessel, the order of the watches, the monotonous, workful, violent life. I liked living out in the weather. Ships satisfied whatever aesthetic instinct I had. I used to listen to the older seamen with the attentiveness of a disciple, and in a short time I had grown skillful in my calling. When I had been two years at sea, on board the *Jacob Thompson* our Swede bosun asked to look at my knife because he wanted to examine the pigtail of square sennit I had put to the handle so that I could haul it out of its deep sheath without a struggle. "That's delicate work. How long you been going to sea?" I hesitated to tell him how little salt water I had sailed over. "I know. You don't want to say you're just a water rat like me. I made my first voyage as cabin boy when I was five years old. We come to Bremerhaven and I try to walk home to Sweden." I felt guilty at taking credit falsely, but I was delighted that the bosun, who had shipped in sail, should mistake me for a veteran. And since I was young, it was from the vantage point of my office, as the Spaniards call it, that I saw all the world. I took for my own the lines of my shipmate, Juan Soto Galán, the ones that end his poem on Helen of Troy:

All talent is kin. What she cannot help,
The naked knife of her glance—
Leapt from the sheath to the hand, from the hand to the mark—

Is like the careless way I turn a splice,
Better than any rigger's loft ashore,
Or read the ship hull-down on the horizon
And tell my wondering mates her name and port.

I took those lines for my own, satisfied that the craft was manly, but now that carpenter, a fellow man and a substantial one, had suggested to me that it was not fully manlike, that it excluded something essential. The suggestion was painful and luminous. If after the war we had not sold most of our ships to the Greeks and the Norwegians, and registered what was left under flags of convenience, no doubt I should have been a seaman to this day. It's no easy thing to find good work, work that one is suited for. But when the carpenter spoke I understood that the life I had embraced was, in my own terms, no more than half a life.

That realization, unsettling as it was, concerned a relatively narrow train of conduct and custom. It knocked me off my pins for a time, but it was a long way short, in its unsettling effects, of the story in the Chekhov collection. That story, which I have compressed to the point of distorting everything but its import, though I could recite it at much greater length, and, I believe, very nearly in the words of the original—except that I will not introduce a work of art on a grander scale than is called for in an account whose proper business is with a modest item of literary history—that story, I have said, has been with me for many years. It made at once the same impression of painful enlightenment that the carpenter's words, his tone, the expression of his face, had made upon me, as if I had suddenly been enfranchised to suffer understandingly what I had hitherto borne unaware. But it was very much more powerful and lasting, a kind of astonishment of discovery possibly equal to the change occasioned by the shepherd's words in the soul of that wanderer in the Sparrow Hills. In both cases the prophet's ignorance as well as his knowledge vouched for his saying. But what the shepherd said struck me as more impersonal in its application and not to be eluded. Chekhov, out of the *trop plein* of his energies and passions, and out of the pessimism of a dying man — for he was dying of tuberculosis — had composed that threnody for his world. And that world was indeed ready for death. In a quarter century it was dead. It is a universal assumption that the world we inherited from that time is a dead world. Naturally we ignore the fact. Life has always been hard, no doubt. But to live in a dead world calls for a ceaseless tautening of the imagination that has made us a race of hysterics. However, that is by the by.

I told Avrahm Yarmolinsky how I had come upon the Chekhov story in my college course years back. I made no reflections upon it. I was meaning to ask him if he knew of the collection in which I had found it, or any other that contained it, since I wanted to read it again. But at one point in my detailing of the incident I began to falter. Something in his manner had made me lose the clue of my thought. The current of sympathetic attention that flows from the listener to sustain the speaker had been suddenly interrupted. Yarmolinsky's grave face was stony. I felt that before I was aware of what it meant. But then experience told me what was about to happen, and I began at once to feel ashamed, like a man caught out. The first instance of it that I can recall consciously had happened some years before, when I was working for Jack Steinberg in the one-horse publishing firm that he later made into a notable house. He was about to entrust some copy-editing to me, and he asked me if I knew what to do with commas and periods when they occurred in the neighborhood of quotation marks. I answered bouncily with a homemade formula. Jack was a passionate man who habitually spoke gently. He was easy to work for—indeed, endlessly indulgent. And I used to feel rather reassured than not by the glint of iron under his affable habit. This time his expression changed abruptly. He said, "Here's *The Chicago Manual of Style.* Take it home, go through the whole thing, so you'll know that it covers everything. And the index is complete. Don't go near that manuscript till you have some idea of what the questions are and where you can find the answers." But I had known myself to be inexcusably at fault before he spoke, simply from the rigidity of his face. And only a few months ago in conversation with a friend, I said casually that I didn't think much of a science of clinical psychology that had changed the definitions of psychosis and neurosis twice in my lifetime. My friend is a physician, profound and droll, with a manic comicality of invention; in discussion a playful tiger. Now all drollery ceased together. His face set, he told me that those definitions had not changed, and he quoted the textbook formulae. What I had meant to say was that their meanings had changed, since they were being applied to clusters of symptoms that were in practice regarded in quite another way than they had been when the definitions were first adopted. One indication was the discovery—less than twenty years old—that neurosis is not the monopoly of the middle class, and psychosis not the specialty of coarse natures lower in the social scale. But I could say none of that, for my friend's face was implacable. I think of Marlow in *Lord Jim*, consulting the French naval officer about the moral bearings of Jim's case, and being much heartened by his ready understanding of the natural fear that had overcome the young man. And so Marlow finds the courage to ask, then, if he is not disposed to take a lenient view of Jim's conduct. And the Frenchman scrambles to his feet, as if eager to keep his garments from contamination by the possibility of leniency, and announces the judgment of his entire nation upon the matter: There is still the question of honor. And as for what may come when honor is forfeit, he can offer no opinion because he knows nothing about that. Implacable. Though I think he is in the right.

Yarmolinsky said quietly, mournfully, "There is no such

story of Chekhov. Almost every scrap attributable to Chekhov that is of literary significance has been collected. That story is not in the corpus."

I understood that the judgment could not be appealed. Yarmolinsky had edited Chekhov, written about him. And I am unreliable about literary sources, my acquirements in such matters being a late growth. But that I should mistake the authorship of a story that corresponded to my buried premonitions of the meaning of my own life, that I should be wrong about the gray binding and faded blue lettering that I had borne for years like a weight upon the heart—had I ever been inside that library, did I attend that college?—these things seemed astounding. Learned men have erred. But then, it could not be Turgenev. I had read *A Sportsman's Notebook* over and over. And it was not Tolstoy or Gogol. And of the small number of Russian and Soviet writers with whom I was familiar, it was inconceivable to me that the author of that sketch might be anyone but Chekhov.

IN THE week that has gone by since my credit card was rejected in the restaurant, I have received the monthly statement of account. From that statement it is clear that if the company had allowed me to charge my restaurant bill of $10.09, there would still have been a balance in my favor of over thirteen dollars. I won't use that card again. I don't like to pay interest to capricious people. I've read that one of the credit card companies, I forget which, has issued fifty million cards. A number of that magnitude guarantees many chances for error, but it also makes discourtesy routine, and suspicion business as usual. How often I've tendered a card for some small purchase, and the clerk has reached under the counter to get the closely printed booklet, and run down the columns of figures to see if the man standing before him is to be regarded as a citizen or a pariah. I used sometimes to pretend ignorance. I would ask, "Are those the good ones or the bad ones?" Usually the clerk would seem a bit taken aback, even embarrassed. "The bad ones." "And have you found any yet?" I never spoke to a clerk who had. But some said that at other counters, elsewhere in the store, or at a branch in another borough, a bad one had turned up. I dropped the game after a while. Those were the terms on which the clerk earned his living. I had thought to educate him about his relations with his fellows, but that was presumptuous. If I had accomplished anything, it was to add a drop of bitterness to his cup.

But it's like trying to give your check for a purchase in a department store. In this city you must produce your driver's license or no soap. Once I had my passport with me, and I was curious to see if the spread eagle and the Great Seal of the United States of America, and the endorsement of the secretary of state, and my photograph—bearded, however—and my signature would turn the trick. No. I had to produce my driver's license. "Patience," my father says when I confront him with things of the kind. But I had a French friend once who used to exclaim on such occasions, "*Quelle époque!*" More pointed and more heartfelt. For our nerves are raw from the climate of affronts and suspicion that we have accustomed ourselves to endure. I go to some lengths myself not to add to the miasma rising from the marsh. Many years ago, a man named Hardesty, from Wilmington, Delaware, borrowed ten dollars from me in a Southern port. He didn't mention that he was shipping out next day. He had been cadet master of our class at the school in St. Petersburg, Florida, where we were to be dubbed (wonders of the war!) ensign, second lieutenant, or third mate if we passed the courses. On our very first evening at the school, while we were in formation in the street outside our barracks, Hardesty had awarded me ten demerits—thirteen meant expulsion. He said, textually, "That will cost you ten demerits." We had been laughing at a mild joke an officer had made; my laughter had gone on a hemidemisemiquaver too long. I said, "That will cost you more than that." And I stepped out of the rank to strike him. But the officer, a lieutenant named Sargent—a very decent man—said quietly, "Stop, mister." The honorific mister was an earnest of my prospective translation to third mate. "Go back to your formation."

In my three months at the school I never collected the last three demerits, so I was duly graduated as an officer in the merchant marine. Hardesty was too. (I believe he had no demerits whatsoever. How would he have come by any?) Four months after that, both of us happened to be in New Orleans, waiting to ship out. I came upon him in Bourbon Street. I think we had not spoken since the night he had awarded me ten demerits. He said, "I'm flat broke. Lend me ten till Saturday." Since I detested the man I could not refuse him the money. And he was gone next day. Recently I told the story to a friend of mine. I told him that by accident I had just learned that there were people of that name still living in Wilmington, that I was going to go there some day and get back my ten dollars with interest. My friend said, "Don't talk like that. Don't even think like that." Now, I am opposed to capital punishment. I can scarcely imagine a nastier custom than allowing public functionaries to assume our responsibility for condemning and murdering a human being. But I have nothing against private vengeance—though I would think it reasonable that my fellow citizens try to restrain me if they believe that I intend an act of violence.

But what was I to make of the announcement, on the part of a scholar in the field of Russian letters—specifically an editor and biographer of Chekhov—that the volume I had read as a class assignment, containing the story I have mentioned, was not by Chekhov at all? Of course, Yarmolinsky did not say precisely that. He simply denied that the story I had told him in summary had been written by Chekhov. Well, I made nothing of it. If the theory of the heliocentric organization of the solar system were overthrown tomorrow, I should be very much interested in the new ingenuities that science was substituting for the familiar ones. But of course one expects some such overthrow. And science does not demand of us a slack-jawed faith in its proposals, just a provisional acceptance of the presumed state of the art, so that investigation may proceed. The Chekhov story is another matter. It happened to me. It is part of my life. I made nothing of Yarmolinsky's denial. And there is a further oddity in all this. Why hadn't Yarmolinsky told me the true authorship of the story? He knew Russian literature as the dog knows the coverts, as at one time, a pilot of the Hudson River, I knew the courses, buoys, lights, and landmarks from Ambrose Light to Albany. It is not credible that in my desultory reading I had happened upon a wonderful Russian author unknown to him. That seemed scarcely more likely than that some writer entirely foreign to Russia would set his sketch of the end of the world in the Sparrow Hills, and report it as a colloquy between a muzhik and a gentleman. I could make nothing of Yarmolinsky's denial.

The poet M. L. Rosenthal is steeped in Chekhov. Not, I imagine, because he takes him for Aeschylus or Shakespeare, but because there are strains in that music that touch his heart. I understand that very well. When I was young, it was Auden, not Yeats, who touched me most.

Yeats was the bigger man, Auden the more clubbable—not that his throwaway manner is without a kind of diffident nobility:

> England to me is my own tongue,
> And what I did when I was young...

In any case, Rosenthal is my friend, and some years after Yarmolinsky had set me that puzzle, he happened to speak of Chekhov's *Ward No. 6.* There's no doubt about that one, at least. And then he mentioned the film that the Russians had made of Chekhov's "The Lady with the Dog." I had seen that. For a few moments two middle-aged men thought of Chekhov, his plays, his stories—and the plague that those stories have unleashed upon us because their atmosphere of things unresolved, of less than heroic pain, can be evoked readily enough by writers who have no genius. And one thing leads to another: I told him my Chekhov story. He said he had never read it. He was surprised. How could one miss a story like that? He would look for it.

But he never did unearth it. He said later that it sounded like something that Chekhov might have written, but apparently he hadn't. At least he himself could find no trace of it among the editions of Chekhov that he had looked through. He wondered if it might not be another writer.

Yes, but who? The problem is rendered more acute by the scantiness of my information about Russian authors. If I know of no more than a dozen, how can I possibly make a mistake? Reviewing them while counting on my fingers, it is clear that none of them except Chekhov could possibly be the author. Well, Gorky and Isaak Babel are remote possibilities. But Gorky did not take that view of life. To introduce the shepherd's monologue somewhere in a story—that would be possible for him. But to make it the high point of a sketch designed to express an intuition of cosmic failure is simply not Gorky. And Babel writes in saber strokes. The impractical-seeming parries that guard cheek and flank, the florid moulinets that are nevertheless the shortest route to an opening, the sudden attack with the point—these make a wild skirling music, an exuberant Totentanz. He would never let a peasant speak connectedly, collectedly, so long a speech, one that gave no occasion for explosive satisfaction in bitterness. Now, I am not even remotely a scholar, but in these matters I have a certain flair. I told my friend—the one who said I must not dream of spilling Hardesty's blood—that in these matters I had absolute pitch. He said, "In these matters no one has absolute pitch." Of course. But absolute pitch is relative; some people are tone-deaf. I have relative absolute pitch, and I will not abate my claim any further, because I have a duty to the truth. And it's a small enough talent that I claim. It would seem that I haven't a shred of imagination. And I can't even read Babel or Gorky or Chekhov in their own language. But the Chekhov story cannot have been written by either of the others. It might have been written by Turgenev, but I have read no other stories or sketches of his except those that figure in *A Sportsman's Notebook*, and it is not among them. How can I be mistaken when I have too little information to make any confusion of the kind remotely plausible?

Certainly ignorance can lead one into error sometimes, and sometimes into sin. But this is not that sort of occasion. I know because I have been led into both, and I can recognize them. Once, for example, when I was on the *Jean-Baptiste LeMoyne*, south of the Florida Keys, I made a serious mistake at the wheel. We had been steering southeast, and the mate told me to come right easy, meet her, and steady her on one-eight-nine. We were making a long plunge into the Caribbean. I carried out the order and reported, "Steady on one-eight-nine, sir." He said, "Keep her so." He left the wheelhouse and went up the vertical ladder to the flying bridge. I heard him stride across the deck above my head. I assumed he meant to take an azimuth of the sun. Then he called down through the speaking tube, "What is your heading now?" I had looked up involuntarily when I first heard his voice, and I looked at the gyro compass again. "One-eight-nine, sir." He asked me the same question two more times in the next two minutes. The compass did not go a single click right or left — the sea was calm — and each time I answered confidently, "One-eight-nine." Then he ran across the deck above my head, tumbled down the ladder, and came into the wheelhouse on the run.

He stared at the compass. He said, "Your heading is one-nine-four." I looked. That's what the compass said, and I had been certain that it had not moved. I had been reading one-nine-four as one-eight-nine, steering five degrees off course. He said, "You deliberately tried to fool me." My shame at having wandered from the course kept me from understanding the accusation. He said, "You tried to make a fool of me." When I could speak, I said, "I'd be a fool to try that. I made a mistake. You were taking an azimuth, weren't you? You had the gyro repeater right under your nose." That wasn't polite, but I was terribly rattled. He said, "You tried to make a fool of me. I won't forget that." To be unskillful was bad enough. To be taken for a cheat and a liar was nearly unbearable. There was nothing more I could say. I thought bitterly that I was the best sailor in the watch. It did not even occur to me that he may have thought so too, and could not account for my being off course during long minutes, cheerfully answering one-eight-nine the while, unless I had meant to mislead him. We were to load oil in Aruba for Valparaiso, but from Aruba we carried the oil back to Perth Amboy, so that the voyage was over in three more weeks. That was lucky. When I signed off the vessel, I said to him, "Mister mate, I misread the steering compass. There's no excuse for that. But I wasn't trying to fool you." He said, "I know what you were trying to do." And that was that. It has troubled me for thirty years, and not because it was the worst mistake I ever made. I've done worse things, all right. It's that the man thought I had lied about something I would never lie about. Since then lovers have said I lied about things one doesn't lie about, and the accusation has hurt less. Men and women are not to understand one another. But that ship's officer and I were members of the same craft. There was nothing to misunderstand. I have never forgiven him.

Here is an odd thing. That man could not be persuaded, years ago, because he had been disappointed in his expectations. A good helmsman stays on course, and if in heavy weather the ship's head is nearly ungovernable, he meets her on each swing to keep her as much as possible from ranging, and tries to average his course—as a young man I heard with a curious elation that "govern" was related to the Greek word for "rudder." And many years later I am obdurate about that man because he felt that I had broken the bond of faith that sustains us all. He was a good seaman, and he should have known my heart by his own. At one time a woman who had a tenderness for me nevertheless found that every action, every gesture of mine, was an offense. I asked her, "Why did you choose me, then?" Her answer undid me: "Everyone lives in a dream of love." The most painful lines in *Don Quixote* turn on the grim joke of our illusions. The don is at last persuaded that what he had taken for a castle and for noble courtesy were hired lodging and professional hospitality. He says, "This is an inn, then?" "And a right good one," the innkeeper returns with perfect satisfaction. The don says, "I have been sadly deluded all this while." The Spanish is more virile and more hopeless — *"Engañado he vivido hasta aquí."*

It must be for reasons like these that I feel an unlikely twinge of resentment at Avrahm Yarmolinsky for having denied my testimony, and at my friend Mack Rosenthal. It is as if they sought to dispel a kindly illusion. No doubt they could not consider what the result might be if they succeeded, since they were themselves testifying to their best knowledge. They were testifying to what they knew, and we owe one another just that.

Now, Rosenthal is a remarkable poet, and the measure of it is that he is, statistically speaking, insane; an essential part of his trade is to conciliate his generation, but he takes no interest in the job. Hamlet says of Osric, "He did comply with his dug before he sucked it." Yes, but Osric has got on, hasn't he, and at the end of the play he is hale and hearty, and in a position to commend his services to Fortinbras. Rosenthal has no such gift. Like every real poet he has had to invent a new language, but his language is unacceptable to the nation we have become. It is not hieratic, remote, like the language of Stevens. It is not a fit vehicle for sly, poisoned confession, like the language of so and so. He doesn't know how to talk tough, like the tribe of the terrified tough. The most noted of his fellow poets are a generation of Malvolios who have had greatness thrust upon 'em. He has no talent for that. A painful case.

He has courage that he would do well to keep out of his verse, courage of readiness and courage of compunction. I was lunching with him one day at his college. Holding our trays before us, we were in line to pay the man at the cash register. There was a foreigner ahead of us in line. He was confused, and the man at the register was insolent. I turned away, mentally, from the business. I'm a modern American. My motto is, Don't look at me—I just work here. I paid, and waited for my friend to join me. He said in a low tone to the man at the register, "I heard what passed between you and that man. He's a foreign visitor, a guest of the university, a guest of the country." The man at the register said something negligently exculpatory. Mack said, "That won't do. I'm going to see to it that you won't be impolite to a stranger again." I felt embarrassed for my friend. He seems to think he lives here, not on Mars or on television.

Another time we had lunch at the White Horse. As we entered we saw a big fellow sitting on a stool with his back to the bar, his elbows braced on it. He was heavy-bodied, with a sunburned face, and his nose looked as if someone had broken it for him not too long ago. He was drunk. He seemed to find us amusing. I excused myself to make a phone call and went past the end of the bar to the public phone. While I was dialing the number I heard Mack's voice. I glanced over that way, and things didn't look right. When the phone had rung five times I hung up. I steamed over to Mack and said, fatuously, "Do you know this man?"

He said, "No, I don't. But he seems to think that he knows me." "I know you," the man said, and he laughed. I turned to him, but Rosenthal took my arm and said, "Let's go into the other room." We did, and we ordered our lunch and the house's infamous half-and-half. Suddenly Mack said, "My God, it's Delmore Schwartz. I didn't recognize him. He's gained a lot of weight, and he looks as if he's been in a fight. I have to apologize to him." With great difficulty I kept him from doing that; in Schwartz's condition it would have been a mistake. "That's terrible," Mack said. "I never recognized him. I'll have to find someone who knows where he's living now, and write to him." I had always thought of Delmore Schwartz as the man who had at the outset the essential gift that most of the poets who were his exact contemporaries never chose to demonstrate, the ability to make a great line. He made only a half-dozen of them, but they are perfectly diagnostic for poetry. One would be enough – "The scrimmage of appetite everywhere." That line is Dantesque. So I was thinking that on my meeting that extraordinary man I had tried to edge him into a brawl.

But what I had begun to say is that Rosenthal is magnanimous and not sentimental, and he can't seem to keep the first quality out of his poems, nor inject into them a saving dose of the other. In sum, he lacks a decent respect to the opinion of mankind. On his head be it.

As might be imagined, those traits make him an inconvenient friend. I get back at him as best I can. He admired, rightly, Horace Gregory's version of Catullus's *"Nil nimium studeo, Caesar":* "I shall not raise my hand to please you, Caesar. Nor do I care if you are black or white."

I brooded on that, and the next day telephoned him to say that I had made a better version: "I couldn't care less about pleasing you, Caesar. You can be white or black—it don't make me no nevermind."

There was a pause. Mack asked, "And did you introduce the ungrammatical expression in order to conform to the original?" I said loftily that I had employed an American idiom to render in a contemporary mode the unbuttoned impertinence of the original. "I see," he said. "Would you repeat the lines for me? I'd like to write them down." So that one missed fire. I doubt that it will stop me, though. I have observed that experience does not teach, though it may canker.

But what it comes down to is that, with less reason to do so than Avrahm Yarmolinsky, since he has not like Yarmolinsky devoted a good part of his life to a scholarly investigation of Chekhov, and with equal lack of concern for the possible consequences to me, Rosenthal has concluded that I am mistaken, and in an unimportant way, about the authorship of the Chekhov story. That, from a close friend, strikes me as cavalier. On the basis of an investigation that could not, in the nature of the case, be systematic, let alone exhaustive, he has decided that I am not to be believed on this point—indifferent to him, capital to me.

IN THE SPARROW HILLS

Now, the trouble with being alone in the world, in the sense that no one agrees with you and the world's experience does not ratify your instinctive feelings, is that you go crazy. I do not mean in a statistical sense. Since no one agrees, you repeat, you exaggerate, you shout. And at last you shout not from outraged conviction but from terror, from distrust of your feelings, since they are coin that does not pass current and you cannot rid yourself of them. At that point you understand that you are crazy. And a man is a social animal. How can you believe that you are in the right when everyone knows that you're crazy?

When I was second mate on the *Ulla Madsen* I invented a method of finding longitude at noon. It came to me suddenly on a day when I was taking the usual noon sights to establish the latitude—just as once, when I was a child riding on the subway and seeing the lights of the tunnel slide by, it came to me that motion in space was the graph of time, and time elapsed the measure of motion. For hundreds of years men had been measuring the angular distance of the sun above the noon horizon, applying a correction for the date, and setting down the result as their latitude. Longitude was a very different matter. To arrive at it one worked cumbersome problems in spherical trigonometry, or, more recently, with one's sight entered volumes of tables and in about ten minutes could hope to come up with a "line of position" that gave an estimated longitude that was close enough for the purposes of a vessel that could not run into danger any faster than fourteen knots. But a dozen or so entries on a form are required, and petty calculations, and there is plenty of chance for error. It came to me that at one moment of the day—noon—one could find longitude almost as one finds latitude, almost by inspection.

Every deepwater ship carries two timepieces, the ship's clock that is set approximately to local time, and the chronometer that is set as precisely as may be to Greenwich time, with its rate of error written down in the log every day after comparison with radio signals. You start to take sights a few moments before noon by the ship's clock, and note the time of each sight with a watch set to local time. The sun is climbing to its greatest altitude, and the successive sights show a larger and larger angle with the horizon. At last the sextant shows a smaller reading—and you know that the sight taken just before that one represents high noon. From it you get your latitude, as usual. Then, by comparing the ship's clock, showing local time, with the chronometer, set to Greenwich time, correcting only for the moments elapsed since that penultimate sight, you have your longitude. The sun passed over Greenwich before it passed over your head, and the difference in time between those two transits is the measure of your distance from the prime meridian at Greenwich—which is longitude. The only calculation required is to change time to degrees and minutes of arc, at the rate of fifteen degrees to the hour, for that is the speed of the sun's apparent motion through the sky.

At first I wondered why the books did not mention it. I must be wrong. Or perhaps it was because the method is usable only at noon, when the sun is on your meridian. But that did not seem a sufficient reason, since the navigator's "day's work" required him to shoot the sun at noon in any case.

Well, I never had a skipper who let me use that discovery. There had to be something wrong with it, though it sounded right. I used the method secretly because it was quick. And since it is inherently more accurate than the method of looking up tables and making entries and manipulations on a form, every day I had to nudge my noon position on the chart and ease it over towards the old man's. But that is an old sea-custom anyway.

Many are the persons I have told of my discovery. Always they looked sympathetic and skeptical. The more they knew of the subject the more careful they were to look sympathetic—*on ne badine pas avec l'amour*—but they were skeptical. I bore it all. Then, last summer, I picked up a yachting magazine on a newsstand, for I love boats and shall never have one now. In it there was an advertisement for an electronic pocket calculator that would solve various problems in navigation and piloting. My eye went down the list of problems disapprovingly: I detest those machines. All at once my heart jumped. You know how it is when you miss your footing on the stair. The first you know of it is that your hand has seized the rail—your body knew the danger before you did, and your heart has jumped. One of the items read "Longitude by Meridian Altitude." The technical term means one thing only. My method, my rejected method is now so much a matter of course that it is programmed on a pocket calculator. And for thirty years I had thought myself mad.

So when my friend Mack Rosenthal adopts with me the tone of a man visiting a sickroom, and says it sounds as if it might be Chekhov, but it appears after all that it isn't, he cannot possibly know that his tactful tone is an exacerbation. He is driving me to the verge of recklessness, something to which my unfortunate temperament lends itself in any case. So, too, is my other friend who is nameless here because he does not properly figure in the foreground of the account I have to render—the one who tells me, "In these matters no one has absolute pitch." After these excitements of my reason and my blood, and given a certain instability which is after all my business alone, though it is probably patent to that small portion of the world that knows of my existence, I think it will be understandable if I do something characteristic and out of character. Then who will be mad and who will be sane?

THE THIRD person whom I must introduce here for the sake of his testimony is Mr. Monroe Engel, who is well enough known as a scholar and man of letters, I trust. He is quite as well known as is agreeable with honesty, and no grander notoriety would serve my particular purposes. I met him three years ago, when both of us served on a literary jury. We had two prizes to award. One of these went, as of right, to the foremost American novelist—now in his dotage but who served the Republic well while he still had all his marbles. The question was, what younger deserving writer should be granted the second award? It had been decided by a kind of unofficial consensus to bestow it upon one who deals in the necrology of our dead world, taking his cue from a hint in T. S. Eliot regarding rusted iron, stonecrop, merds. And that made me think of another and most gifted writer who was still blindly evoking memories of life, the possibility of tragedy. Then I did something unseemly, for I know how to sway a committee: a child's heartbroken insistence, or the calm lucidity of the paranoiac, or a new proposal put forward with manly firmness when everyone is looking at his watch and thinking of his luncheon engagement—these are features of my armamentarium. I think none of my fellow committee members understood the willfulness of my filibuster in favor of vanished hope, except a young woman—herself a notable writer—the youngest member of the committee. She understood because she is hostage to death by reason of her youth, with her teeth set against vain sentiment. But she was outvoted.

After the formal session there were a few minutes of conversation, and Monroe Engel spoke to me. He was cordial, as if I were a man and a brother rather than a person secretly convinced that his literary passions had more than a tinge of defensiveness. And we are a social animal; Mr. Engel's manner made me feel readmitted to human converse. Our discussion before the vote had provoked the mention of Chekhov, and Mr. Engel told me now that he was editing a collection of the stories. I told him of my Chekhov story. I asked if he was acquainted with it. In putting the question I tried to disguise my eagerness to be delivered of the burden it has come to represent to me. He said he hadn't come across it, but that he would be reviewing the entire corpus, and he would let me know if he found it.

People say those things, but life intervenes, and you do not hear from them. So I was touched to get a postcard from Monroe Engel some time afterwards. I have it before me now — the only physical document in the case:

> January 8
>
> I've not been able to find the Chekhov story you described. Perhaps it will turn up in the one volume of stories (the stories of 1894) that has not yet been issued. If not, you have a collector's memory.
>
> Sorry not to be more helpful.
>
> Sincerely,
> Monroe Engel

A collector's memory. That is an interesting coinage. Under other circumstances I suppose I should think it pleasantly witty, signifying the substance of things hoped for that cannot possibly exist. I am in any case very grateful to Monroe Engel for his courtesy, and I hope he will not think it an ill return that I hale him before the public on my business without asking leave. For my need is great. I am too old to imagine that the volume containing the stories of 1894 (my father was at that time a child of five) will sustain my claim. Besides, more than two years have passed. Mr. Engel has no doubt finished his review of the Chekhov corpus some time ago. I am sure that he would have let me know if he had come upon the story.

Now, that puts me in a very difficult position, though I might appear to have sought it. I may resent—not on trivial grounds, but on grounds that are scarcely avowable nonetheless—Avrahm Yarmolinsky's ukase in the matter, and the pronouncement in the same sense of my friend M. L. Rosenthal. The fact remains that I appealed to their special knowledge, and they answered me according to their understanding of the case, as they were bound to do. Marshaling their testimony in this account has been painful to me, but I have gone through with it doggedly. Monroe Engel's report I cannot resent at all, though he has delivered the latest blow to my hopes. The problem is severe, and it is not simply a matter of my having been hopelessly wrong about a literary ascription that has had special meaning for me. I have been wrong in worse cases and survived. I mentioned how Mack came to the defense of a foreigner—unknown to the man himself, simply on principle, because that man was the stranger within our gates. Well, I have had very different relations with foreigners in my time. I shall not dilate upon an incident in a Latin-American port where, one night, drunk and about to be arrested (for cause), I snatched the policeman's saber from its sheath, foined at him with the point to gain a moment's start on him and his companion, ran along the wharves in the darkness, came on a providential *lancha* with oars in her whose painter I cast adrift, pulled away towards the anchor lights of the shipping in the roadstead, made my own vessel at last, having run into the stage at the foot of her lowered accommodation ladder, discovered the accursed sword still beside me on the thwart—the pommel gouging my hip and the point jammed under the stretcher against which my feet were braced—hurled it away from me into the water, and from the stage spurned off the *lancha* to drop down-current, all with no thought of the policeman who was answerable for that saber nor the waterman whose livelihood was that boat. That happened far away, in a far-off time, and I had the excuse of being drunk and frightened. But not long ago I was crossing Seventh Avenue from the west, and the traffic light changed before I had reached the sidewalk. Immediately I heard the baleful blast of a highway horn at my back, and the car passed so close that I had to jump for the curb. The driver shook a fist at me as he sailed around the corner into Bleecker Street. I began to run, and I pressed on until I caught up with the car at Sixth Avenue where it had stopped for the light. It was liver-colored. When I pulled the door open the driver shrank away as far as he could without letting go of the steering wheel. He was a dark man. At that moment he looked as if he had been hit with a singlejack. I thrust my head and shoulders inside the car and said murderously, "The pedestrian has the right of way in this city." "You cross with red light." Cars that had come up behind us sounded their horns. I felt disgust and savage pleasure at his fear. "In your country, no doubt, a man in a car can run over any man on foot. Don't ever try that again here." I slammed the door, exulting in the noise. The liver-colored car moved away and the next car sounded its horn indignantly at me as it went by. I could scarcely see. For a few minutes I found it hard to walk because I was shaking, and as that began to leave me my satisfaction too ebbed away. The business took on an ugly look. I was ashamed.

No one, I trust, will imagine that I have described here the worst actions of my life. I have done worse things. And the swan's breast stems the turbid flood and takes no stain, but the things of man are otherwise disposed. Every act of prepotence or cowardice has left a sediment in my spirit that darkens for me the stream of life. But somewhere I keep a measure, as they say a meter stick is preserved at Paris to try the truth of all the others. Even in this city that offers no horizon I find out a level and a perpendicular. In the end I know how much things come to, which way is up. To suppose that I would be ashamed to acknowledge that I have been dim-wittedly ascribing to Chekhov a story of which he is innocent, would be to deny me all sense of proportion, as if I could not tell the difference between footlessness and faithlessness. It's true I can't say how it comes about that I should be so mistaken, but I long ago resigned the childish passion for knowing the inessential—if I want to be fully informed I can always read *The New York Times*. It is something else that troubles me. For even as I loathe with all my soul the waitress's musky aura, her hoarse voice, the matter-of-fact brutality that informs her brisk, awkward movements, so I hate the artist's mountebank suppleness of self-exposure, his gift for uniforms and posturing, for being all things to all men, for taking on willingly the tincture of the stream of his times. I know there is in it a certain temporal majesty, marked with grime, as there is grimy majesty in empire or in the vulgar power of Concorde. But it troubles me exceedingly to confess what at this point the reader may already suspect. It was not what I intended at the outset, I could swear to that. But do I know what I intended? And to take responsibility is one thing; to feel myself complicit is another. Nevertheless it appears, against all likelihood, that in a certain season, when day was drawing off, the brown air taking the creatures of earth from their labors, all alone I girded myself for the journey and its pain, and composed—magisterially—the myth of our times. It was a signal and thankless effort, but the mere mention of it has persuaded men of judgment to consider for a moment its admission to the canon. It seems certain now—in my own despite—that I am the author of the Chekhov story. What genius I had then.

A DREAM OF FAIR WOMEN

For John, a stranger,
yet more like than we know.

I SAW HER on the crosstown bus at eight in the morning. Half an hour later the morning rush is at its height, but now there were six or seven passengers only. On entering I had made for a seat nearly opposite the rear door on one of the two long forms that run the length of the bus. As soon as I was seated, I found my place in the book I had with me. I looked up from the page at some point. A woman was sitting across the aisle. She must have boarded the bus at an earlier stop, but I had not noticed her when I came in. She was tall and spare. Her eyes were cast down. I went back to my book.

But there was something not quite right about the picture she composed. That must have been why I found myself looking at her again, examining her absently. She was a handsome woman in early middle age, her clothes were of the plain sort that cost a good deal, and she had a Nordic air—broad forehead and high cheekbones. With her face inclined forward, the lines on either side of her mouth seemed deeply graven. At that angle, too, her upper lip was disproportionately large, blank and featureless as an ape's except for faint shadows as of furrows to come, the first intimations of the collapse of the flesh that elsewhere in her face was firm, with the ruddy skin drawn taut upon it. She raised her head slightly. The deep lines that had framed her mouth disappeared, and her upper lip grew human and comely. Then she raised her eyes. I turned away at once. Of course I did not want to be caught studying her. But I looked away with an impulse that had nothing to do with social embarrassment, for at that very moment I was certain that while she was looking directly at me, she did not see me.

The bus stopped. A young man entered, paid his fare, and sat down next to her. As he did I understood what it was that I had unconsciously remarked in her. She had not been sitting erect, and her lower body was canted far to the right side. I recognized that because when the young man sat down she shifted about, composedly, as far in the opposite direction, not looking up, aware of his presence but not so aware that she altered her lounging attitude—as if she were at home to lounge and muse and not in the lurching bus. That confirmed the shock of her glance. Her eyes in the instant that I had seen them were astonishing. They were very large, intensely blue. They transformed her face with the fulgor of their light, but they had none of the arrogance of beauty that appropriates what it looks at. They had regarded me with a child's uncomprehending stare.

When she had shifted about to avoid the young man, her shoulder had come closer to his. The space marked for each passenger by the hollows in the seat and back of the long plastic forms is not large enough to allow two good-sized men to sit side by side without their shoulders touching. But, her eyes down, she took no notice that in moving away she had moved closer to him, just as though she were alone in the bus, sitting as she chose and not as the custom demands.

Before I got off at my stop that morning she looked up again, not at me but straight before her where I happened to be. Again her glance was like a blow—concentrated as a searchlight, incurious, blinding. And I had to turn away at once. The power of her look was something she could not help, a kind of exposure. Its incomprehension was either vacancy or the habit of defeat. I walked to my office, thinking uneasily of what I had come upon.

About a week later I got on the bus again at eight, early for me, but I wanted a little peace before office hours began. Our business is phone systems, sales and maintenance. The complaints would start at nine. I was thinking of one account and what I was going to say to him. First, one of our men had been to his place yesterday, and he had checked all thirteen units. Every feature of every unit had operated perfectly. A machine of that kind has no temperament, no imagination, no sudden impulses. If you follow the manual — one small page of large print — every feature of every unit has to work. We had had four calls from that account, the very first sarcastic and bellicose enough. I would tell him that we could have all those units out of there in an hour's time tomorrow if that was what he'd like. Here it is the twentieth, but I'd refund the whole month's charges. If he preferred, he could take another month to find himself a more satisfactory system, but in that case I'd have to charge him for the entire period. I was starting to feel better about the whole thing. That's a good system, introduced ten years ago — a long time in our business. It's simple, dependable, and the least expensive one we handle. You feel helpless when you get irrational complaints. Now those complaints were going to stop. By habit I had found the seat nearly opposite the rear door. When I looked up I saw that woman sitting opposite me across the aisle.

I suppose I had not been aware of her because I had been preoccupied with that troublesome customer, but also because she was quite still. People sitting in a bus show signs of life, if it is only nervous restlessness. She was looking down and you could not tell that she was breathing. I had not remembered that her hair was brown. The severe plan of her face was contradicted by that formless expanse of upper lip with its faint shadows. As she began to raise her head, I saw with satisfaction how the lip took its place in the design, and I knew that now she would raise her eyes. She did, and that bolt of impersonal light blazed upon me for a long moment, perhaps even after I felt that I must look away. Then the odd pose of her body struck me again. After all, money had been expended on her upbringing. She was no longer of an age to be lolling unselfconsciously in a public place, like an adolescent wholly absorbed in herself. I thought she must have the habit of unhappiness. It occurred to me that I could ride two stops farther than usual and still be no farther from my office when I got off the bus. She must live in our neighborhood, because I get on two long blocks from the end of the line, and only the near one is residential—the other is all warehouses and auto-repair places. I could speak to her. My wife would know what to make of her, she has an instinct for life. But at that point I overheard myself thinking. I had been going on as if I owned all the women and was responsible for their welfare. I had made a professional diagnosis and was preparing to get a second opinion from a specialist. In fact, I had seen an opening for a good man.

We were just then approaching my usual stop. I rose hurriedly and left the bus. Since that day I have been feeling less pleased with myself than I like. I learned something that I would just as soon not know. It's as if I had been reading one of those parodies of human conduct—say, *The Kreutzer Sonata*, or *Notes from Underground*, or even *The Egoist*—that make you feel guilty of abominations. Well, fair enough. In the abstract we are all guilty of being alive in a terrible world, and we kill to live. What is unbearable is that you recognize the portrait, not as something abstract but as a likeness of yourself. I would not have been so solicitous for that woman if she had not been at once *comme il faut* and impossible. What an opportunity, the force of beauty rendered imbecile. And the mere guess at the possibility that that might be the case with her (of course it was no more than a guess; how can we know immediately a soul by its envelope?) had been enough to make a conviction of it for me. I had seen an opening for a good man.

I have been thinking ever since of my long service in the wars of the sexes. With what blind good cheer I had borne my part. How many times, cut to the brains, I mended, and, professionally courageous, went back into the line to deal out strokes that showed a practiced arm. Those old passwords, honor, duty, loyalty, have been hardening my heart for a lifetime. Those old seductions, promotion and the promise of loot, gave the final touches to my character. And a career of that kind begins so lightly—lightly as each of its episodes. I have been thinking particularly of the incidents of a two-year span long ago. It is our subtlest sense, our gentlest fiber—sympathy turned appetite—that betray us to have another go each time our enlistment is up. We are made that way.

When the outfit was disbanded, the valid men went to rifle companies as replacements and the broken crocks were scattered anywhere. I was among the crocks. My orders were for counter-intelligence, Stateside—an error, since I had the wrong makeup. In those days I was a patriot. I expected the land of the free and home of the brave to act the part. Naturally my America hurt all the time. But makeup or no, I learned things while snooping for the Army.

Within a few days of my arrival at the detachment I was sent out into the city to develop information. Subject was Nancy Knowlton, nineteen years old. I was not told what sort of information was wanted, nor why. I asked the case control officer. He had not been told either. "Just run down the appropriate list of questions." Well, it's hard to frame a question if you don't know what you're looking for. It's hard for Informant to answer if he doesn't understand the questioner's intent. But I was to have no intent. That made me uneasy the first few times. I was to have no intent and Subject was to have no politics. Some weeks later I wrote in a report that Subject—a different one—was thought by his neighbors to be a registered Republican. The case control officer said, "Don't put that in. You're not mad at him, right? Maybe they're just giving him security clearance for a job. They don't want to see any evidence of zeal."

"Not even Republican zeal?"

"No zeal."

But on that first day, when I went out into the city to subvert subversion, I was clad only in my innocence and brandishing a sling. I went straight to a shop owned by one of Nancy Knowlton's references. References, there's another study. Mostly, references are on the side of the investigator (they assume he has an intent) and against their own friends and neighbors. Instance, a reference of mine, a buddy, told the Army that he could not affirm without qualification that I was loyal to our country. How's that again? Yes, that's what my friend said. A woman friend testified that my sexual proclivities were indeterminate—that was her expression, it was right there in the report. And I had thought all the while that she was in a position to offer a more positive judgment. In the process of vetting me for counter-intelligence, a panel of officers guyed me about both those bits of testimony, and I was glad that they found the situation amusing. If they had been humorless the business might have been awkward for me. In my outfit a good man, son of the Yugoslav ambassador to the Court of St. James's and member of a social class that had been abolished by the revolution, had been denied his security clearance on the ground that the country of his birth was now communist. Too bad. He was a first-rate soldier, and the best argument for a ruling class I ever met. I hope he flourishes.

As it turned out, Nancy Knowlton's reference was on the

side of her friend. But then she made odd-looking shoes, no doubt good for your posture, out of what appeared to be Pará rubber. She had blocks of the stuff about the place, cubes sixteen inches on a side, smelling sulphurous. She was a surprise, a regular baptism of fire in my new military occupational specialty — middle-aged, precise, one of those practical persons with an absent air, and something more. When I showed her my Special Agent's card, she said at once, with a courtly gesture, "Come in, young man," as if that document were a letter of recommendation from a distinguished personage. She directed me to the settee and perched on the stool by her workbench.

"If I may, I'd like to ask you a few questions about Nancy Knowlton, who has given us your name by way of reference." As I said those words I looked up from the blank pocket notebook that was supposed to keep me in countenance. Even before she answered I felt the hair prickle at the back of my neck as if I had heard the Scots pipers skirling away among the guns at the battle of El Alamein.

"Nancy Knowlton. The young. The young. We lose our hearts to them — and they break our hearts."

It was spoken coloratura. But it wasn't stagey or ridiculous — the lady was more an antique Roman than a Dane. And those words were the first true things I had heard in some time. I had not expected to be talking *Menschlichkeit.* The questions I had mentally prepared seemed pitiful. I was in a false position, and yet decorum demanded that I not embarrass her with my embarrassment. At last I said, "May I ask how long you have known the young lady?"

"Five years. We met when she was a junior counselor at a summer camp where I taught arts and crafts."

"And the acquaintance was kept up after that?"

"Friendship rather than acquaintance. Affection on both sides, you see, and esteem on both sides. As happens sometimes despite great disparity in age and in temperament. But latterly it's quite fallen away, one hardly knows why. These things have their seasons. Their natural history of growth and decay, I imagine."

I did not know how we had arrived where we were. I fell back on my prepared questions.

"It would appear that Miss Knowlton is being considered for a position of trust and responsibility with the United States government — "

"Ah, is that so?"

"Yes, ma'am. That is, it appears so. And I'd like to ask if in your judgment she is a person of good character." My voice trailed off at the end. The inquiry sounded so like an insult.

"Beyond question. She is a young woman of excellent character."

I took down my first professional note: "Excellent character." Of course. The better to break your heart with. The world seemed less hospitable than it had yesterday, when

Subject was simply a name and reference number in a dossier.

"You regard her as reliable and dependable?"

"Most reliable. Most dependable."

I wondered if the government would be pleased. There was a suggestion here of something approaching zeal.

"You have found her a quiet, steady young person?"

"Oh, no. Very animated. And absolutely trustworthy. Upright. Candid. With the kind of moral intelligence that immediately distinguishes the better and the worse." Her glance moved about the room in a review of Nancy Knowlton's virtues.

"You make her out to be a most unusual young woman. That is, she seems very young to have so marked a character."

"One in a thousand. Charming manners, even when she was a mere child. Charming voice. Most interesting turns of speech. Most original mind, and not at all clamorous for attention. Delightful to look at. Lovely slim figure, fine bright face—vivid coloring, you know."

Nancy Knowlton, what have you done?

Undone two souls, at the least reckoning. I have not forgotten you after a quarter of a century. How willing we are to be enchanted. Hadn't I caught at the very start of that conversation the note of ideal beauty—not the girl's only but the grown woman's as well, she of the Pará rubber shoes and the spirit avid for the ideal? Against my will, pained and embarrassed by her emotion, hadn't I played to her exquisite connoisseurship of beauty, provoked her to speak, so that her account of that young woman's mind would be transport and vastation for us both? Surely I had. We are made that way. And there's no telling what headquarters and still higher quarters eventually decided about Nancy Knowlton, but I think it certain that the authorities took her up by the wrong handle. My report, conceived in the required bureaucratic categories, could not have helped them. I did not say that she was one of those dangerous persons who inspire devotion. The report ended with the ritual formula, "No unfavorable information regarding subject has been developed to date." And that allowed all hands to reserve judgment, which in this case amounted to reserving judgment on an incendiary. But perhaps the authorities were fireproof. Perhaps they were insured.

One day I was ordered to conduct an interrogation of a suspect. Those things always come out of the blue. I was to go to a certain building, room number so and so. To my surprise, I found two of the men from our detachment there, and they told me what they had been told. Suspect worked in a sensitive facility. On entering the country he had presented a British passport that the British now said was fake. Suspect denied it, but he had told seven different stories to support his denial. So he must be up to something. In fact, he had come to the attention of counter-intelligence because he had told at least as many stories to his American girlfriend, all of them engrossing and contradictory. Not without reluctance she had turned him in to us. The interrogation room was next door. Suspect was waiting in there for my arrival. I was to attempt to find out what his nationality might be by trying him in whatever languages I knew. After polite preliminaries, I must switch on the recording apparatus, and my fellow agents would be listening in from right here—there was a convenient receiver for the purpose. Afterwards, we would compare notes.

Suspect was a sandy-haired man. He might have been in his middle twenties or his middle thirties, precociously mature or belatedly boyish. He seemed pleasant enough. When we had lit our cigarettes, I turned on the recording machine.

First I asked his name. "Ian Parker. Surely you've seen that famous passport?" I told him that the British were quite firm in their opinion that the passport in our possession had not been issued to him. "Yes, so I've heard. Absolutely preposterous."

I asked what his occupation had been in Britain. He said that he had been cutting timber in Scotland for nine months before he came to the States. That was a new one. And, with his slight build, it was hard to see him on one end of a two-man saw.

"Are you a Scot, then?"

"No, English. Work is where you find it, isn't it?"

He had me there. He went on to give me a picture of the logging operation, with a wealth of technical detail. There was a single jarring note. He said, "Working around heavy equipment is a heads-up business." A year earlier I had read that line in a story about a logging accident. In its context, that line was striking. I was sure that it had struck him.

It occurred to me that possession of a false British passport was not conclusive evidence against Ian Parker's being British. But I had to assume that he had already been questioned minutely about his life and times in the United Kingdom.

He was fluent in French. He told me that he had done his military service in the French army. He had been *caporal chef* in an infantry outfit. I asked him what model of bayonet went with the issue rifle. He gave me the model designation and the length of the blade in centimeters. It sounded reasonable. Then he remarked that he thought it a detestable pattern. *L'arme blanche*, cold steel, was serious business. On that particular bayonet the blood gutters (he said *gouttières de sang* as if he had said nothing else since boyhood) were very deep and ran from the quillons very nearly to the point. The purpose of the gutters was to make a T-section and stiffen the blade. But they were forged too deep. He had no confidence in the strength of that bayonet. While he was offering those observations he kept his cigarette in the corner of his mouth and talked past it, Frenchy.

He was perfectly at home in Spanish. He had worked in a fishing village on the Costa Brava, putting up mullet roe. He briefed me on the manner of it. I told him I knew that stuff and had a weakness for it. He said that I wouldn't if I had worked at preserving it. And he pronounced the Spanish word for "preserved mullet roe" with the careless air of an old preserver. I asked him if he knew the name for it in French; there is one, as there is in English, but it is almost as rare. If he knew it he would most likely have read it in Rabelais—which might have meant something or other. But he didn't know it.

Then we tried Italian. Then German. Then back to Italian because I had heard something in his music. He was interested at once. But as soon as I had heard it again we dropped Italian. I wanted to lead him elsewhere and take him by surprise.

"You've been here nearly two years. How come you don't speak American?"

"I can if I want to, chief. But I'm English. I'm allowed to speak my language my way, right?" His accent was a hatefully accurate version of my native woodnotes. We both laughed. While he was still laughing I said in Swedish, "Tell me your name, quickly, don't stop to think."

"*Jag heter Ian Parker.*" His Swedish seemed authentic to me. And "Ian Parker" came out as a Swede innocent of English might have said it—if there is such a Swede. He looked at me, and after a moment he laughed again. The worst had happened to him, and yet his adversary was no further advanced. "I can do that in Norwegian and Danish too."

"So can most Scandinavians."

"Yes, and some English."

Now, the tactics of argument—and of interrogation—are never to concede a point, never to recognize that the other man has the initiative or the right of way, just forge ahead like a brute. Rearrange the universe by taking no account of what he says. Make him dizzy. I'm no good at it, but I tried again. I asked him what jobs he had held in Russia. He struck his cheek with his fist and shouted, "Ouy!" I really don't know how to represent the noise phonetically, but it jarred me, because you couldn't invent that gesture and exclamation. One would have to have learned it from a native, preferably Mother. He went on in Russian, telling me that I was no mere polyglot but a cosmopolite, cultured and therefore formidable. He was way ahead of me, and by now really enjoying himself.

He had rather enjoyed the whole business. He was an artist, and he had found someone who could appreciate his performance. He was a child, delighted if he could get a grown-up to watch him skin the cat. He was a touching madman. Even if he guessed what might happen to him if he were to keep it up, he was powerless to stop. He had learned that way of getting through the world. Those pertinent fictions were the man.

"Are you a seaman?" he asked in Swedish. "Did you learn your Swedish on Swedish ships?"

"I learned my Swedish on Norwegian ships." My answer was impatient, and I didn't care if he took it for rudeness. When you understand that you're in the presence of a victim, you think of his fate and begin to hate him for it. Caught up in that mood, and sick at his being so pleased with the talent that had put him in the soup, I began to talk to him severely. After all, he was a prisoner. I was interrogating him. That made me his moral superior.

"Listen to me carefully. As far as I can see the only concrete thing that stands against you is that you entered the country with a bum passport. And like an idiot you talked your way into having them check up on your passport."

He looked as if a connection had been made for the first time. "Did Helen — "

"And you're about to talk your way into a federal prison. I would guess that you're Scandinavian, but it doesn't matter. You can make up stories in any language. If you can't control yourself, if you simply must invent a new world every time you're asked a question, you've had it. But if you can manage to keep your mouth shut — just go back to the first story and stick with it — the worst they can do is deport you. If you go on making up new stories you're going to convince them that you're dangerous. Out of all the stories you've told, they'll pick out pieces that seem to fit, and those pieces will make a story that will get you put away.

This is wartime. The last thing anyone will believe is that you're a harmless lunatic. So your only hope is to act as if you were sane.

"Now, if you tell anybody what I've just said to you, it won't do you a bit of good, and it won't do me any harm. I'll explain that it was a ruse."

"Are you telling me the truth?"

I turned away disgustedly. He said immediately. "No, no. I know you're telling me the truth."

But when I had turned, I had seen for the first time in many minutes the red signal light glowing on the recording device. We had been on the air all that time. Me, who had always been crazy about everything electrical. I had been bemused by his virtuosity. I had forgotten where I was, what we were doing.

I turned the machine off. Then I said to Ian Parker, "Don't throw away the chance you have. It's going to cost me a lot."

I went out of the room and closed the door behind me. It seemed that I could see straight ahead of me only, and the arc through which I could see kept shrinking. I thought I made out my two fellow soldiers sitting at the desk where I had left them. Then they rose and came towards me. They were smiling awkwardly. "How did it go? We missed the last ten minutes. The machine's on the fritz."

It was a while before I could answer. "I think he's probably some kind of squarehead. But I'm sure he's a harmless nut. He can't help telling lies. The best thing to do would be to boot him out of the country for passport fraud. Can we make any suggestion like that?"

They looked at each other.

"You could put it in the report. But you know things like that get edited out."

"I'm going to say it's my strong belief that he's mentally ill."

"You can try. It seems a shame for him to get into big trouble if he's just a nut. But are you sure?"

"If I could speak Chinese he'd have told me in impeccable Mandarin that he'd worked in a lacquer plant in Peking."

But I needed to sit down.

Three months later I had my honorable discharge. Four months after that, in April, I ran into one of those fellows. I asked him what had happened with that Limey. He said he didn't have the details, but Parker had been tried and sentenced to Leavenworth. "He was pretty bitter about you, you know. He said you pretended sympathy for him so as to gain his confidence and then betray him." And my man gave me an odd look.

Some two years before that, in a January thaw, I was one of a knot of men standing outside a storage building in an Army camp. We were recruits. I had been named platoon guide because I had the requisite military bearing and was by far the oldest—most were eighteen, some were seventeen. We had been marched here to draw our weapons, and been abandoned outside a locked door. We had been in the rain for an hour. Since I had official standing, I was the target of questions before five minutes had gone by. "If I knew the answers I wouldn't be here." And I meant that because I had tried for the Signal Corps and had come up infantry. I didn't mind fighting, but I preferred to fight near a radar device, a radio, a field telephone, anything that offered a little interest. Then the men started to make jokes. But no one came and the rain-soaked fatigues were cold on the skin. Everyone grew silent. The smokers were afraid to smoke. "Hey, can we have a smoke?" I pointed to the only distinguishing mark on the blank façade in front of us, the stenciled No Smoking. They stood around in the rain, their shoulders up, their necks pulled in, sighing from time to time, infant philosophers.

Yesterday had been rather jolly. Lots of hectoring, but we had drawn our bedding and our clothing. With the big duffel bag hitched to one shoulder, and a rolled mattress riding on the same shoulder, we had slogged half a mile through the mud to the barracks. For some of the youngsters, it was their first experience of a real burden. Their faces showed terror as they tottered under the load. Some dropped their gear, convinced by the pain that they could not carry it. But they were encouraged with bellowed threats and insults. And once in the barracks, there was the agreeable mystery of bed-making to master and the fun of stowing away all the new stuff in the footlockers. Then the bugle sounded mess call — "We're eating like kings!" — and then there was Care and Cleaning, which meant visiting around. An easy day for the troops.

But today we were drawing our weapons. And at last someone came hurrying up, a corporal. "All right, men, you're cold and wet. Sorry about that. Something went wrong. But we'll be under cover in a minute. Column of ducks!"

We formed twos, and once the lines were neatly dressed he unlocked the door and marched us in. There was a long counter with a row of naked bayonets upon it, and beyond them a row of bayonet sheaths. The corporal lifted a hinged leaf in the counter and placed himself behind it. "Men, the artificer sergeant's been delayed. I have to give you a little orientation in his place. These are your bayonets. They're not toys. They're not meant to dig with. Don't toast bread on them in a bivouac. Almost certainly you'll never see a bayonet charge. But the bayonet's a desperation weapon now. All it's good for is to save your life. Abuse it, take the temper out of it, it's useless. You can see they're all shined up now — keep them like that. First man! Pick up your bayonet and file along to the row of bayonet sheaths. Right. Pick up your sheath. Right. Next man!"

At that moment the door was flung open, and a man wearing sergeant's stripes came into the room. He came in complaining in a hoarse voice, moving fast along the counter, drunk and raging. I stepped back from the counter to give him room. The man behind me in line was looking at the artificer sergeant in surprise and did not step back in time. The drunk man said, "Out of my *god*dam way," and struck him with his shoulder as he went by. The boy fell to the floor.

You know the impulse to pick up a fallen man. People will try to do it even when a man's been hit by a car. I had the bayonet in my right hand, the sheath in my left. I dropped that sheath before I knew what I was doing, bent down, grasped the boy's arm near the shoulder and hauled him up. When he was steady on his feet again, I turned toward the sergeant who was trying keys in a far door beyond the end of the counter.

"How would you like to knock me down, Sergeant?"

The corporal said at once, "Soldier, put down that bayonet!"

I had forgotten it. I took a step forward and slammed it onto the counter.

"Wouldn't you like to knock me down, Sergeant?"

The corporal had moved over to where I was, with only the counter between us. He said firmly, but not very loud, "Trooper, knock it off. We don't talk like that in the Army. In three months' time you'll get all the fighting you want. We fight the enemy—we don't brawl with one another."

He was stating the ideal. Quite right. For an instant it did seem to me that he had overlooked a detail: the senior soldier present was drunk on duty and had knocked down a recruit just out of his teens. But if the senior man misbehaves you have to find order and discipline in yourself. Quite right. The corporal was invoking that principle so that I might escape the stockade here and die usefully anytime now in a war I did not care for. Well, that was inconvenient for me. But he knew how we ought to live, and I took it kindly that he had gone to the trouble of explaining it to me.

"Pick up that sheath."

I picked it up smartly.

"Sheathe your bayonet. Hang it on your web belt. It'll be there or hooked to your pack whenever you're under arms. Right. Next man!"

When we were all accoutered he led us through the inner door. The artificer sergeant had disappeared, but he must have unlocked the long rows of rifle racks before taking off.

"Men, as each of you files by, I'm going to read out the rifle number stamped on the receiver. I want you to repeat that number to me. I won't let the rifle out of my hands until you've repeated it correctly, so's you can begin to memorize it. After that you're responsible for your rifle and responsible for its condition. You must remember your rifle number. Now, a man gets to recognize his rifle because every one is a little bit different. But when you take it from the rack, you check that number anyway, make sure you're right. And if you've stacked arms in the field, when you take the stack apart, you check that number. The reason is that you don't want to pick up a weapon one day that some fool has neglected, and lose your life for it. A better reason is that it's a part of soldiering, and from now on until the time you've been discharged or you've bought the farm, you're a rifle with legs onto it. That's what you have to be if you're going to fight, and it may help you come out alive. First man!"

When we had our rifles the corporal took us outdoors, formed us in ranks, and showed us order arms and right shoulder arms. Then he marched us back to the barracks. He counted cadence, chanting,

> GI beans and GI gravy,
> GI wish I'd joined the Navy.
> Am I right or wrong?

We already knew the answer to that one, and in good humor we shouted, "You're right!" as the right foot came down.

"Am I right or wrong?" he persisted, pleased with our pleasure.

"You're right!"

And on the beat he swung into,

> The corporal rides in a jeep,
> The sergeant rides in a truck,

The general rides in a limousine—
But we're just out of luck.
  Am I right or wrong?
  Am I right or wrong?

And so we reached the barracks.

"Platoon—halt! Order—arms! Dismiss. Good luck, men." And he turned away.

What an excellent young man. In the barracks, I sat down on my bunk and began to examine the unlovely Garand rifle. I was thinking about the corporal, and then, without transition, of the scene a week ago when the draft was being sworn in. There was a dandified sergeant at a large desk. His uniform shirt had been altered to represent his satisfaction with himself, and he looked as if he had been sewn into it. He handed me a long document. "Read it and sign it."

It took a while to get through. It required me to swear that I had never sought to overturn the government by force and violence, and had never belonged to any of a surprisingly long list of organizations. I recognized a dozen perhaps, but there must have been several hundred in all. Well, a test oath is offensive to a patriot. But while I hesitated I knew that I was not going to refuse to sign it. And I did sign it. And I was directed to move towards the group that was waiting to be officially sworn in. Before I reached it I heard, "Why not? Because I'm an American. I don't sign things like that. I've been called up and I'm ready to serve. But this is the United States — I don't put my name to things like that."

Someone said, "Call the captain."

"Call the general if you want. The government wants to know if I've been a good boy, does it? Well, the government can ask my mother. I don't sign anything of the kind. This is the United States of America."

I could not make him out clearly among the crowd at the desk. In a minute or two an officer came, and then he went away with several men, the man who would not sign among them, I supposed. I was feeling pretty sick at having been found out. Perhaps I hadn't known what I was doing, but I certainly knew now what I had done. I had missed a chance to behave that would never come again. And for the man who had exposed me I felt only resentment. He had done something embarrassing in public. Thinking about him now in the barracks, I knew that I had just seen his counterpart, that corporal. What fine young men.

THE boy I had pulled to his feet in the weapons hut told his father how I had saved his life, offering mine for his, and other wonders. It turned out that his father had been a schoolfellow of my father some time around the Civil War. They had lost sight of each other years ago. Here they were, both of them living in the same city. What a coincidence. They must meet. Benny's father had a daughter two years older than her brother. Benny's father had money. He imported Egyptian cotton, Turkish tobacco, and some natural gum used in printer's ink and ice cream. The daughter had independent money because she had inherited a pile from her mother — and the latter was still alive-o. The two fathers decided that the girl and the hero would make a splendid pair. Her father said her heart was in pawn to baseball, football, and hockey, but a likely young fellow could set that right. My father said that I might fit that description once I gave up my passion for electrical gadgets and gillhickies — a little ballast was what I needed. The girl, her mother, and her father were all to pay Benny a visit on post to congratulate him on his hairbreadth escape, and things would take their course.

But before the parade happened I got a message to call a number, collect. I remember phone numbers, and I couldn't imagine why A. would shout me to a free phone call. At the Message Center I saw my first push-button phone — what luck that it wasn't in use; all the rest were dial phones — and I spent some time working out how the circuits might be arranged inside the case. But then I had to hurry up and ring him because the men in line behind me were growing impatient. A.'s girlfriend was pregnant, and did I have any money? No, but I knew where I might be able to borrow some.

In the barracks I asked Benny if he could lend me three hundred dollars. I had a friend, and his girlfriend was pregnant. Benny assumed that I was my friend, but he was a man of the world, and he felt close to me. "No, but I've got a weekend pass. I'll borrow the money from my father, give it to you Sunday night."

Sunday night his manner was altered. Had I blotted the page with his father, mother, and sister because of my indiscretion—being my own friend and all? No. It seemed I was still eligible.

"But do you have a car?"

"A car? No."

"Do you have a boat?"

"No. What's the connection?"

Well, if you had a car or a boat it would be different."

"Are we talking about the same thing?"

"Well, for collateral."

"Collateral? If I had collateral I'd go to a goddam bank for the money."

"My father just doesn't see how he can help you out." He looked unhappy.

"That's all right. Thanks anyway."

And I called B., who also assumed that I was my friend, but he was sympathetic and solvent. He'd send me a check right away. And he did. And about a year later, though I had sent him installments out of my pay—A. had other expenses—he was the one who chose to tell the Army investigator that he could not in conscience attest to my loyalty to the United States. Figure that one out.

A DREAM OF FAIR WOMEN

In any case, on the day that Benny's family visited the base, they pulled a rifle inspection on our company. I come from a family of soldiers, and parade-ground drama is my idea of a good time. Already I had twice been chosen Colonel's Orderly because I was so good at inspections. Of course, being platoon guide helped. I was the first man in the rank, and the inspecting officer generally assumed that I knew how to play, so I had more than my share of opportunities. This time, we had a surprise visit from a general and a group of Canadian officers. The party strolled over from our right front. We came to port arms. The general, a short, chesty man, made as if to pass and whirled suddenly to confront me. I was ready for him. In the millisecond in which he squared up, I bobbed my head down like a mechanical duck, flicked a glance into the rifle's open chamber to inspect it for that not impossible cartridge, bobbed my head perpendicular, fastened my gaze on his forehead, and began to drill through it. By the time his right shoulder stirred I had his pineal gland precisely in focus, and I knew he intended no feint but would take the rifle. As his hand touched it, both of mine shot away from stock and fore-end to gain my trouser seams. He looked at the breech, the receiver, the barrel. For all I cared he could look at the butt plate or down the muzzle. My genetic makeup guaranteed that the piece was immaculate, just as my boots and brass were effulgent, just as I knew at what instant he would thrust my weapon back at me. My hands came up pat as he did, and by the time he had let go of the rifle it was again at a Euclidean port arms.

He barked, "How do you like the Army, soldier?"

I barked, "I prefer civilian life, Sir."

Concentrating on his pineal gland, I was nevertheless aware of the hypothalamus and the ganglia in the foramen. I could see he was in no way at a loss.

"Why is that, soldier?"

"Greater opportunity for the exercise of initiative, Sir."

"That's correct as far as your experience of the Army goes. But your experience is limited to life in a training regiment. Once he's out of leading strings a smart soldier finds occasion for initiative everywhere. Sergeant! See that this man gets a three-day pass."

That was the longest speech I ever heard at an inspection. And it was delivered at parade-ground volume. A triumph for the general, for C Company, and for the platoon guide.

And Benny's family, a discreet twenty yards off, had got the good of it. Once the sergeant had seen our weapons put away he told us to go chase ourselves, and Benny and I marched to the encounter. His mother was a rosy, pleasant-faced lady, an excellent augury for her daughter. She took my hand in both of hers, which were soft. After all, I was a man who could make the bad world say uncle for her little boy. Benny's father gave me a manly handshake. "I've heard a lot about you." Clearly, he was a good winner. He didn't hold it against me that I had failed to beat him out of three hundred dollars, American. Benny's sister was a lively young woman. And she was in fact taken up with baseball, football, and hockey, as I learned in the course of the afternoon. She put intellect and imagination into it. Well, that wasn't unsympathetic. I could understand fanaticism—I had built a pretty good record player, mostly out of salvage, when I was twelve. Then why did I find her so hateful? She was guilty by association; she came from the wrong set of loins. Her father was a democratic pluralist. I could populate the globe with bastards for all of him, and still wed his daughter, as long as I didn't fool with his money. So all afternoon, while being attentive to that young woman, I was preoccupied with one thing: what had my father been thinking of? He had met that man forty years before I had. He must know what his old schoolmate was like.

On that three-day pass I asked him the question. Tactfully, of course. He was taken aback.

"Don't you think she's a nice young woman?"

"Well, yes, as far as that goes. She didn't ask me for collateral."

"To tell the truth, he was always a little like that. I'd forgotten. He was a year younger, so I didn't see all that much of him. But aren't you being a little unfair to the girl?"

I laughed. "You mean by not going after her money?" I can't say anything that crude to my father without apologizing for it by laughing.

"Well, let's be serious for a moment. For now, there's nothing to lead us to suppose that she's anything but perfectly decent. She works somewhere, and I understand that it's a responsible job. She has a great deal of money. And her father displays business prudence amounting to crassness in matters that you and I would regard as requiring a certain delicacy. Isn't that right? So that's how it stands on the one side.

"On the other, you're my son, and I'm very fond of you. Sometimes I think that at bottom we look at things the same way. But you have no profession, you have no trade, you have no outstanding talent, you have no prospects. That is, you're going to have to get through the world under severe handicaps. And yet you repine at the thought of marrying a rich young woman."

Of course I had always known that my father felt more or less like that about his son. He had a sterner—and more joyful—view of life than it was given to the men of my time to entertain. He was in fact fond of me, but he could not think me fully human, so frivolous, dissatisfied, and uncommitted I seemed to him. And I was very sorry to disappoint him in that way. But there had been no crisis like the possibility of an advantageous marriage ever before. He had never had occasion to say what he thought. And his words troubled me a lot. I suppose that was why I managed to see more clearly what it was I shrank from—the possibility of ritual contamination. And I didn't see it until the answer was out of my mouth.

"Dad! It's me that's going to have to sleep with her."

His face changed. There was a sense in which he had not thought of that. He was silent. And he never alluded to the subject again. He felt that if I had done him that violence I must have been very upset. The truth is, he and I are more alike than he imagines.

On the night I was back in barracks after my pass was up, a fellow from another company came in with a duffel bag full of submarine sandwiches. I asked him if they were any good.

"So-so. You can eat them if you're hungry enough."

"With a pitch like that, you must sell a lot."

"Listen, don't kid yourself. C Company's at the game now. Wait till the game lets out. I'll sell every one I've got. I don't have to beg anybody. These are mostly young guys. As long as they're awake they're starving. I buy them for half a buck, I get a buck and a half."

"How many do you have in that bag?"

"A hundred. I'm going to town once more tonight, and I'm coming back with another load. Two hundred bucks a night, no sweat."

Benny had been taking it all in. He drew me aside.

"Why can't we do that?"

"What for?"

"Make some money. You're always broke, aren't you? Here's a chance to make a little money. You put up half, I'll put up half, and we'll split the profits."

"When I say I'm broke, I generally mean I have no money. Don't you have fifty bucks?"

"Sure."

"Well, what do you need a partner for?"

"That bag must weigh forty, fifty pounds. Didn't you see him struggling with it?"

"Okay, advance me twenty-five, and you take seventy-five out of the profits."

"But what if we don't sell them all?"

"That's investor's risk. But I'm tired. I'm not as young as you sprouts. Find another guy. Try the sergeant. I think he has the makings of a businessman. He sure can't drill worth a damn."

"I think I'll try it alone."

What had my father been thinking of? I was angry at Benny's sister, as if she had assaulted my virtue. And it was perfectly possible that nobody had told her that she was supposed to grow old along with me. A few years later, my own sister told me the news. That girl had married a Greek shipowner—it was in the paper. My sister was sardonic about the match. No girl was good enough for her big brother. She said, "Deep calleth unto deep." As for me,

I felt relieved, just as if the two families had not drifted apart meanwhile, and the threat had been ever-present. The curse of trade attaches to everything it touches.

This is what I did to Bill Clancy, my comrade in arms. I give him that grand title not because we had sworn *Brüderschaft*—he was a man of sensibility but not given to emphatic gestures. It is rather that I so thoroughly approved of him. And what I did may not sound heinous. I can't forgive it. As I see it, that small matter is steeped in the elemental faithlessness of the world, just the thing that Bill was incapable of having commerce with. Commerce in other, vulgar, acceptations—that's something else. The first time I heard the expression "I can get it for you wholesale" uttered seriously, not as a joking reference to somebody else's crude attitude, I heard it from Bill. He didn't think any acquaintance of his had to set up to be the big butter and egg man on a spree. It was sinful to consume one's substance paying full price for anything, with the accompanying tax to the middleman. The Corps gave us agents a small sum to buy civvies with, and for the money I had found not one but two suits in a loft somewhere. The first time I wore one of them to the office, Bill said, "Looks good. I hope you didn't blow the whole allowance on it, though." I looked hangdog, so that I could enjoy his surprise when he learned the truth. "Why didn't you tell me? I can get that sort of thing wholesale."

"I got two of them with the money."

He brightened up at once. "Well, good for you. You never cease to amaze me. You look like an infant, but now and then you show glimmers of sense."

Not so one of our captains, the nice one. He said, admiringly, "Good-looking suit. What'd you give for it?" His Pennsylvania Dutch lilt made even that friendly question sound ironic. I told him the price. "Really?" You could have got a new one for that." I never could remember that the serpent cooed like the dove.

Bill came to notice when we were classmates at the counter-intelligence school. A visiting colonel delivered a lecture in the assembly hall. He spoke to us of our high mission. He warned us that the enemy would go to any lengths to subvert our integrity. In that connection he drew our attention to the case of Albert Einstein, master of duplicity. And he went on for five minutes about that arch-fiend in human form.

Bill rose to his feet.

"Sir, may I ask a question?"

"Certainly."

"Are we against Einstein because he told President Roosevelt that we ought to make the atom bomb?"

"We don't know his motives in doing so. But that is not what I had in mind."

"Sir, are you suggesting that Einstein is a commie?"

"There is some evidence for that which I am not free to

divulge. But that is not the ground on which I would censure him."

"Sir, is it because Einstein is a Jew?"

"Certainly not!"

"I ask because I'm Irish myself. I have a lot of sympathy with people who can't stand an Irishman. So I thought perhaps—"

"Soldier! What is your name and rank?"

"Colonel, I am instructed by higher authority to answer all such questions as follows: My name is William A. Clancy, Jr. I regret that I am forbidden to reveal my rank. However, I am authorized to say that it is fully adequate to the mission I am fulfilling at this moment. If you need to know more precisely, may I respectfully refer you to the Commandant of the Corps, who will give you complete satisfaction."

Here we were still in school, and Bill had found an occasion to deliver that mouthful, officially, to a colonel. Heretofore we'd only been able to try it out on our classmates. I don't remember how that hour ended. To me, Bill's getting up on his feet in the crowded hall, coming to attention, and putting his questions to the colonel had a heraldic, chivalric character that I thought wholly admirable. One of the ordinary vicissitudes of life, Blimp haranguing the troops in a way that would be thinkable nowhere but in a hierarchical organization—the Army, any corporation, any school—and Bill had made it his business to show a sign of life. I joined the group that had gathered around him after we left the hall. One fellow said, "Jesus, Clancy. What'd you do that for. Can't you see he's a nut?"

"Listen, this is a matter of public hygiene. If he's got any deep, dark secrets, let him tell us. Piss on that hinting around."

"Yes, but a bird colonel. You're in for it now."

"Well, I don't know. But it doesn't make any difference. If a man talks like that he ought to find out there's a price to pay."

He was always like that. On the same post one evening they were showing a movie with Grace Kelly in it. Someone said something disparaging about her. Bill said, "That's not so. You shouldn't say that. She's not like that at all."

"How would you know?"

"About five years ago I had a job as lifeguard at a place on the Jersey shore. She spent that summer there. I was her boyfriend for the summer. She was really nice. That sort of thing doesn't change. She was a fine girl and I'm sure she's a fine woman."

I was glad when we got orders for the same detachment, though it was in his hometown and not mine. One Saturday in fall we went after rabbit and pheasant. He borrowed a gun for me, a nice old Lefevre double. I said I'd bring the shells, but he said he had four boxes from last year, and you didn't want to keep those things too long. I forget how he arranged to be the one who took care of lunch. In the morning he got two rabbits. I hadn't had a shot. In the afternoon we tried the soybean fields, and after an hour of marching and countermarching, a pheasant got up in front of us. It was a surprise, because pheasants prefer to run, and just at that place the cover was thick enough to give them concealment at a little distance. Bill called, "Your shot!" It was anybody's shot. I said, "You take it." "Shoot, dammit!" I fired, and some feathers flew, but the pheasant sailed on. As soon as Bill saw that there was lead in the bird, he took off. He ran some seventy yards, jumped a fence—I said to myself, Bill, you shouldn't ever do that with a loaded shotgun—bounded across a dirt road, and pounced on the pheasant right at the edge of a wood where it would have been lost, probably to die. He brought it back and tried to hand it to me. I told him it was his bird. I hadn't made a clean shot, and he had run after it when I hadn't had the presence of mind to do that. He said I hadn't made a clean shot because I had delayed, waiting for him to shoot. Also, if you took an animal's life you'd better eat it. "Otherwise it's just slaughter—you know that." I happened to agree with his casuistry, but I asked him why he couldn't eat it himself. "I've got two rabbits. This bird's yours. Come on. We'll quit now and get some coffee, what do you say?" He was always like that.

The year after, I was out of the Army, working in an office. Bill phoned. I was very glad to have news of him. He said he kept running into guys from the detachment, since he lived in that town. He had run into Gewurz, one of our captains, a real I-spy type, mean, credulous, and infatuated with his role of guardian of the Republic.

"That must have been a treat."

"It sure was. He gave me the high sign. We went directly to the boys' bathroom—taking separate routes—exchanged secret messages, and swallowed them. Haven't seen him since."

He said he expected to be in town in three weeks' time. "How about lunch?" And we made a date.

This is what I did to Bill Clancy. On the morning of our appointment a woman called me at the office. She was distressed about us. She wanted me to come and talk to her. I didn't want her to be any more unhappy than she was, and I wanted very much to see her. So I left the office—it was around eleven—and didn't return until three. A Mr. Clancy had come by for me at noon. I was too ashamed to call him at his home that evening. I never called him. I have not seen that gallant heart since then.

WHEN I got to the detachment office in the morning, Bill Clancy was singing pleasantly. He had been put in charge of case control to replace a man who had received orders for Japan, no one knew why. Bill hated any desk job. "I like being outside. Shakes a little up the ideas." So he sang to give himself courage.

> On an April day I walked to view
> The Shannon flowing clear—

Our nice captain said, thoughtfully, "Clancy, I always wished I could sing."

"Uh-huh," Bill said, "and now you wish I could."

The captain was surprised, but he recovered quickly.

"How did you guess?"

"Easy. All your taste is in your mouth." And Bill sang on.

> Upon a matron fair I cast my eye
> With iron bands was bound—

"Clancy! A moment's peace, I beg of you."

"Captain, a man in your position mustn't beg. Have the grace to pull rank and order me to be silent, after the immemorial manner of your kind."

"Very well. Silence while I instruct these young men." Fred Manciple had just arrived, and the captain beckoned to him and to me. We approached his desk.

"You both still unmarried?"

We answered together. Fred said, "As far as I know," and I said, "That's a personal question."

The captain said, "Good. You may have to make a pinch today. Draw your weapons and report here for further orders."

The weapon of the Corps was a snub-nosed .38 revolver. Fred took one with an abbreviated belt holster, because he got to it first. I was left with a shoulder holster, which had rigging a little less complicated than a parachute harness. Fred watched me get into it. "I'd be afraid I might shoot myself if I were wearing one of those." I didn't answer.

The captain inspected our weapons, to see that we had the hammer down on an empty chamber. His manner was slack, most unmilitary, but he watched for things like that. As he had explained once, "It looks bad if a member of the Corps puts a bullet through his foot."

"Now, men, you may very well find all this firepower excessive today. I want you to go to this address"—he showed us a report form—"and interview Mr. or Mrs. Terence Dunn. Subject is John Dunn. He is Terence Dunn's younger brother. If you should find him there, bring him in. And we have no way of knowing that he is not armed."

"Cut it out, Captain. Is he or isn't he likely to be armed?"

"I haven't a clue."

"What is he wanted for?"

"For questioning."

"But sir, we can't just throw a gun on him and push him into a taxi. It's against the law."

"We are directed to apprehend him if we can make a proper identification."

"How do we do that? Suppose he denies he's John Dunn?"

"Ask to see his driver's license."

"This is the craziest thing I've heard yet." I was appealing to Fred Manciple. But he was the steady sort, true blue. He didn't feel that the job was beyond us. I wished it would go away, but Fred just wanted more information.

"Sir, does the report suggest whatever it is that he may have done?"

"In a way. He worked at the arsenal up to two weeks ago. Then he disappeared. No one knows where he is. So the people at the arsenal are nervous. Who knows what he may have been up to? Who knows what he may be up to now?"

"How old is he?"

"Twenty-three."

"This is too much. Some young guy skips from his job, and they send for the Counter-Intelligence Corps. Why don't they call the cops?"

"They did. The police, very properly, referred the case to us because the arsenal is a sensitive facility for the military."

"Sir, do you believe that?"

"No."

"Then why are we going after this guy? And why the guns?"

"We are going after him because we have been ordered to. And the guns are because he may resist, particularly since he is most probably innocent of any wrongdoing."

"That's disgraceful."

The captain looked down at his desk top. He said, "All right. If you won't go, I will."

"Sir!"

"All right, then. Now, if you do find John Dunn at his brother's house I want you to be very careful. As has been mentioned, an arrest of this kind is against the law. An unsuccessful attempt at an arrest is equally bad, in itself and in its possible consequences. I would recommend that you show him your agent's cards and invite him to inspect them closely, comparing the photographs with their originals. Stress the point that you are on an official mission, and in every way try to persuade him to accompany you. If possible, don't let him see your weapons. If you must draw them, don't shoot—unless he's armed and actually threatening you with a weapon. Remember, he's a fellow citizen, and very likely hasn't done anything of consequence. It's bad enough we have to pull him in. It would be worse if we injured him. In fact, if he's really averse to coming along, and two minutes' discussion doesn't change his mind, drop the business and come back here. I'll ask you to keep that part of it confidential."

"Captain, if we're not going to force him to go with us, why the weapons?"

"He may be armed—and angry, or scared, or drunk. I can't send you there barehanded. Now, take your time getting to the house. Think the whole thing out, and make up your minds to avoid a fight. If he's not there, find out what you can about where he might be, etcetera."

"Yes, Sir."

Then we were in the street, walking towards the bus stop. When we got there, no bus was in sight, and since we had been told to be deliberate we walked to the next stop. The bus passed us when we were midway. We waited about ten minutes for the next one. Fred was thoughtful, and I was upset. Certainly the soldier's virtue is obedience. If he doesn't have that, it isn't clear what it is that he does have.

At the same time, if a soldier can't choose he can't have a conscience. I knew that the captain had been the first one to face the dilemma in this instance because he had known of the orders before we had. Besides, he was enough older than we were to make a difference. He had had time to sort things out, so he couldn't play innocent with himself. And then, he and not headquarters had to feel responsible for sending us on such a mission, because he knew us.

"What are we going to do, Fred?"

"Well, first we have to see what happens."

Yes, but the thing about these daytime calls is that nine times out of ten, if anybody's home at all — most people are working and the rest are going about their lives — it's not the man of the house but the woman. The worst thing I could think of was that Mrs. Dunn might be there, and if her brother-in-law had not just left his job but regarded himself as a fugitive, he might be there, too. To go with us would be to put himself in danger. And with the woman there he might be less willing to show himself craven and give up his rights. I said, "I hope he's not there with his sister-in-law."

"I was thinking about that. Chances are he's not there at all. If he's been up to something, he wouldn't be at his brother's, where people would go looking for him. I know that's just logic. But I wouldn't be there, would you? If he is there, the more people in the house the better. It'll pass off easier."

"You think so?"

"I could be wrong."

"But what if he hasn't been up to anything, and he is there?"

"That might make a problem."

THE ADDRESS turned out to be in a block of row houses that were very nearly identical—frame construction, brick stoop, small bay window, outer door of glass with a curtain behind it. The stoop was so narrow that we ascended it in echelon, Fred first. Standing on the top step, he rang the bell. The door opened at once.

"Good morning, ma'am. Fred Manciple, of the United States Army Counter-Intelligence Corps. Here is my identity card, which serves as my credentials. This is my associate. As you can see, he is also a member of the Corps. We'd like a few minutes of your time. We are investigating a matter that is of interest to the Army and to the United States government."

I was a step below Fred. The woman at the door seemed very tall.

"Come in, gentlemen."

The words sounded somehow foreign. She held the door open for us, and we had to pass her in the narrow entryway. When we excused ourselves, she said, "Not at all." We went before her into the parlor. "Do sit down, gentlemen." As we looked about uncertainly she moved toward a wing chair at the far side of the room. She must have been an inch under six feet, but she was so strongly made that she seemed taller. When she turned to us we were still standing. "Do sit down."

Fred sat on the couch, and I made for another wing chair. When we were seated so, we were all nearly equidistant. She gave us a moment in which to compose ourselves, and I looked at her directly for the first time. I thought at once that I had never seen so imposing a person. She sat upright, in an attitude of quiet attention, her hands in her lap, looking like one of the powerful seated women in the Parthenon frieze. Her manner was not stiff, but her form of courtesy forbade anything like cordiality on short notice; she would wait until the two strangers explained themselves. Her black hair must have been quite long, for it made a large whorl at the back of her head. The skin of her broad face and brow had a healthy pallor. I had heard people speak of violet eyes. I saw a pair of them now for the first time knowingly, and they were useless for providing me with a standard. Perhaps this woman's remarkable eyes could be accounted for in terms of their index of refraction, but they seemed to me to be the emanation of a spirit strong, serene, and just. I said to myself, wonderingly, She is Irish, and the trivial discovery resounded in that form in my mind while at the same time I was aware of two thoughts that were scarcely connected. The first was that we were seated in such a pattern that it might trouble her to look from Fred to me and back again in the course of our talk—and I felt the muscles set themselves to raise me from my chair. The other was that I wanted to look at her. I was very well where I was.

"You are Mrs. Dunn?" Fred said. "Mrs. Terence Dunn?"

"I am."

"We are here to make inquiries about your brother-in-law, John Dunn. We would be grateful for any information that you might be able to give us about him. Do you happen to know his age?"

"Yes. He was twenty-three last September."

I wondered at Fred's asking her such a question. She must know that he knew.

"Twenty-three." He wrote it down in his pocket notebook. Then he recited the last address we had for John Dunn. "Were you aware that he was living at that address?"

"Oh, yes."

"Have you ever been there yourself, Mrs. Dunn?"

"I have not. I must tell you that we are not close."

"When did you see him last?"

"I would say about three or four months ago." At that moment she looked at me. I had started to take out my notebook when Fred began to put his questions to her. But I had been disconcerted by their direction and tone, and I had been holding my hand up near the level of my inside breast pocket. Then I had reached in to take the notebook. My hand touched the rounded butt of the revolver, and I pulled it away as if the metal were hot. She had caught the motion and she had looked at me.

"Mrs. Dunn," I said, "we should very much like to know the whereabouts of your brother-in-law. If you can tell us, we need trouble you no further."

"It's really no trouble. But I am afraid I can't help you in that way. I have had very little contact with John altogether. The brothers are not close."

She was looking at me still. I thought, She will tell us nothing. We shouldn't be questioning her. She is perhaps thirty years old—very little older than Fred and I. From her accent, she has not been in this country long. I must thank her so that we can take our leave. And all the while I was looking at her as one looks at an uncommonly fine sunset, with a sort of exaltation that was utterly impersonal, aware that she was most beautiful, but principally because she seemed more fully human than any person I had known.

Fred unbuttoned his jacket. From where I sat to the right of him, I could see the pistol grips riding just above his belt on the left side, for he favored the cross draw. I thought the pistol must still be concealed from her by the skirt of his jacket. But what if he turned? Very likely, just as I had done, he had forgotten that he was carrying it the moment he had realized that John Dunn was not in the house.

Fred said, "You knew of course that John Dunn was employed at the arsenal?"

"Oh, yes."

"Did you know what his job was there?"

"I asked him that once. He said he inspected various parts with a measuring instrument to check their dimensions for accuracy. I remember that because it seemed a responsible post for a young lad."

"At twenty-three, that is?"

"Perhaps I thought of him then as my husband's young brother."

"When did you learn that he had left the arsenal?"

Was it because he was looking at his notebook, reading from it, writing in it, that he put such questions to her? Well, he was thinking his way through the problem of getting her to say something she was perhaps loth to say, or at least of assuring himself that she could not be moved to say it. Or assuring himself that she knew nothing, as we knew nothing.

"I did not know that he had. Rather, I did not know until just now. My husband may know. But we have not discussed it. Perhaps, gentlemen, you might want to come again in the evening, when my husband is at home." And she looked at me to include me in the invitation.

All her words were spoken slowly but without hesitation. She was talking with two strangers, minor officials of some kind, who had a purpose they regarded as serious. She was seriously entering into their purpose as far as she could — or she appeared so — and she was completely, attentively, at her ease. I was sure that the look she turned upon me, willing to be helpful but not choosing to anticipate us nor inquire of us, was the look she directed at Fred as he asked his questions. If she was in fact deliberately frustrating the interrogation, she was doing it effortlessly, as a woman might check the impetuosity of a small child with a gesture or a quiet word. For my part, my impetuosity was checked. I wanted simply to be where she was, to live in that light. But I was feeling ever more insistently that Fred and I were intruders who ought to remove ourselves at the earliest possible moment, not because we troubled her — manifestly we could not — but because we were corrupt. Now, the physical bulk of the woman, the glow of her pale, broad face, spoke of mortality, just as our bodies, Fred's and mine, with the gross health of men who had been spending the better part of two years in the open, were of the earth earthy. Indeed, her weight must have been within twenty pounds of ours. But we were agents, pursuing desire not our own. We were instruments. She was entire.

"Have you any other recollections of things John Dunn may have told you about his work at the arsenal? Or that he may have said to other persons when you were present?"

"I think not. I asked him the one time, and he said what I have told you. I asked him casually, as one does, to be saying something to him. He answered in the same way. Perhaps his work was rather technical, and he thought the details would not interest me, or that I might not understand. In any case, he said no more to me about it than I have told you."

"Would your husband know where we might be able to reach his brother?"

"He may. But John may not have told him where he is now."

"Wouldn't it be somewhat unusual for your husband not to know his brother's whereabouts?"

"Well, there is a considerable difference in age between them. There is also a considerable difference in temperament. It happens sometimes in families. Two men who are sons of the same house may be quite different in body and mind. I have never thought it strange."

She seemed in fact to be considering the matter for the first time—and why not? Brothers are sometimes so different that they would never choose to be acquainted, and they know each other only because of the accident of birth. Yet she had answered Fred without any sensible intention of irony.

"Can you describe for us your own impression of John Dunn, his character, his tastes, his amusements, his acquaintances—anything of that sort?"

I wanted very much not to be associated with his line of inquiry, but I could not think of any way of removing myself from that "us." However, the word was official, and apparently she found it neutral. She took a moment to reply. She looked at me as she began to speak.

"Well, gentlemen, you must know that I have seen John only three times since my marriage. You cannot, I suppose, be asking if I like him or not. He is my husband's brother. And since our meetings have been so few, I have not had opportunity to learn much about him. I know none of his acquaintance. And though he is my brother-in-law, I scarcely know him at all. For any information about him my husband is much more the proper person to speak to."

All this was said without a suggestion of impatience. She did not seem to find us obtuse or impertinent. Even her suggestion that we could not be asking her to define the degree of sympathy she might feel towards John Dunn appeared from her manner as she spoke to be a simple setting aside of a possibility that was in social terms unthinkable — and if that was excluded, then we were again considering matters of fact that, as she had told us, she was not in a position to know. Her eyes upon me, she struck me very much as wondering if she had not missed something in this conversation. What she had missed was the mechanical impersonality of Fred's conscientious pursuit of his duty. She had missed the innocent brutality of it.

Some eight months before that day I had been on a patrol. Two men were detailed to climb to the next ridge and have a look. It was wooded and brushy all the way up. When we got to the top of the ascent, the ridge was flat, and because of the brush we could not see where it fell away again to the next valley. If somebody else had had the corresponding idea, this was not a good place. My companion motioned to me that I should go to the right and then forward again to where the ridge fell away. He would go to the left. It took about five minutes, moving slowly, before I reached the far side of the table. From concealment, I looked across to the next hill. There was heavier growth on its slope than on the one we had climbed. Binoculars would have been needed to make out whatever might be there, and we had none. Then I looked down into the valley. A stream came down from a side hill, and in the valley bottom it ran through a clump of trees. A man was squatting among them, his trousers down, at about two hundred yards. I thought I could see his rifle leaning against a bush. I waited for him to stand up and pick up his weapon. I kept looking away to see if there was anything stirring, and back again at the squatting man. Then there was a shot from my left. The man before me fell over.

The way the fighting had been going, there would be mortar fire coming in on our ridge very soon now if there was anyone on the opposite slope or on the ridge above it. I pulled back at once, and got to where we had first reached the table. The other man was already there. He said, "That's all the patrol for today." I think I nodded. We looked down the hillside and across to the far slope. Our people were in concealment down there. Nothing moved. He said, "Let's not go back the way we came. I'm going to go down on the far side of that spur. You take the other."

A DREAM OF FAIR WOMEN

"All right."

"Couldn't you see him from where you were? He must have been right in front of you."

"I saw him."

"What were you waiting for?"

"Let's get out of here."

"You have any objection?"

"No." I didn't have any. I knew what his reasons were. And I agreed with them, more or less. He was annoyed with me for a while after that, but then he gave it up.

Fred Manciple was being methodical and persistent, doing his duty. But I found myself on my feet. I said, "Mrs. Dunn, you've been very kind. May we call on you at some time when your husband is at home?"

"I'm sorry not to have been more helpful. But I'm sure my husband will be able to answer some of your questions."

I led the retreat. Poor Fred stood up, holding his pen and his notebook, and then he noticed the gun on his belt. He was so eager to button his jacket over it that he forgot to transfer the pen to the other hand. I was glad to have put an end to the interview. I was quite calm. But I felt our leaving to be a renunciation. Why? I had no hope of being promoted into her ambit. Certainly I did not mean to call on her again. Fred could do that without me. But we do not easily quit the place of a revelation. When we came to the entryway I fell back so that the woman of the house might open the door. "Thank you very much." I had to look down only a very little to look into her eyes as I spoke. She was certainly near six feet, broad-shouldered, robust, and not in the least discommoded by being within inches of two strange men who had appeared from nowhere to put questions to her.

"Not at all."

Though we were on a level, and I was looking downward a little, she seemed to me to be the tallest of us. The illusion was physical, not moral.

"Good afternoon, gentlemen."

Fred paused for a moment to look at his notebook again when we were in the street and walking down the block. "Why did you hustle us out of there? You know, things come to the surface after you've talked awhile."

He made another mark, then put up his notebook. To keep her atmosphere about me a moment longer—I needn't have worried, the intuition of her has never left me, not in rage or lust or sorrow—I said, half to myself, "I've never seen anyone like that woman."

Fred turned to look at me. "What woman?"

THE OTHER ROGOZHIN

When I was a young sprout we lived for a time in a neighborhood that nowadays would be described as mixed, or perhaps by some more scientific term that comes to the same thing. But to children not far into their teens the neighborhood is the shape of the world, for all that radio or television can do. At the time it did not seem mixed to me. It is only now that I find that world interesting because of the Irish, the Finns, the one Mormon family fresh from Utah, and the Russian Jews. There were a good many of these last, often with Russian or Russianized names, and some with Russian names that had been Anglicized in the last generation. Benny Baron once showed me a five-kopeck piece that his father, a cabinetmaker, had brought with him from Russia. "*Pyat kopiek*," Benny said, pointing at the words stamped upon the coin. I looked at the Kyrillic letters unenlightened.

We moved away. Five or six years later, during the war, I

found myself in Murmansk and I saw around me the faces of the Jewish boys from my old neighborhood, and the faces of their fathers. (The women, for some reason, were not good likenesses of the mothers and sisters of my friends from that time.) But it surprised me that Russian Jews in America should look like the Russians of that northern port city. I thought of Benny Baron, and Chickie (properly Charlie) Gillel, and Marty Ross, and Bernie Rogozhin. Bernie was an intense, skinny kid. His hands were so small that he could not get a proper grip on a football to throw a pass. He could run, though, and he could catch any pass. No matter what position he was supposed to be playing he was always deep in the other team's territory, yelling passionately for a pass. Olavo the Finn, a natural athlete and born general, would gratify Bernie with a pass only one time in four — there had to be discipline, *Ordnung muss sein.* When I was older and read Dostoyevsky I encountered the Rogozhin of *The Idiot.* Nastasya Filipovna's lover seemed very different from Bernie. However, in a Soviet film of *The Idiot* that I saw long after, the actor who played Rogozhin looked like Bernie grown to dark young manhood, exalted, depressed, and murderous.

Now, I have a friend who is a well-known writer. He has a Russian surname. I am not going to mention that name because what I have to tell is really his story and in that sense a personal matter, and the issue is somewhat delicate. For convenience I'll call him Rogozhin. But you must not think he is murderous. He is decent, affable, sociable, poised, talented, intelligent—a useful citizen. That is why I am taking his story from him. Lou is not his given name, either.

About three years ago, maybe more, Lou visited the Soviet Union as a member of a group that had some cultural business there, of a semiofficial kind. He came to our place for a drink almost immediately on his return. He had brought back walking pneumonia from Moscow—he looked awful—and he had something else troubling him. He said he couldn't shake it off.

Lou said, "The evening of the day we got to Moscow there was a dinner for us, and I was in my hotel room getting ready. There was a knock at the door. I opened it. A man came in, almost pushing past me. He closed the door behind him."

Lou told us that the man had no English. Lou was in the same case when it came to Russian. The man said, "*Ya Rogozhin,*" pointing to himself. Then he pointed to Lou and said "Rogozhin" again. He showed Lou what appeared to be an identity card, but that did not help because Lou did not know the letters. Somehow the man managed to say "Voice of America." Lou gathered that he had listened to a broadcast, the names of the American delegates had been mentioned, and he had recognized the name Rogozhin. He pointed to his identity card and said, "Kiev!" Lou understood that he had come from Kiev by train, a great distance, in order to meet his namesake. The man from Kiev suggested that they might be blood relations, in signs that were explicit and in words that were unintelligible. Lou said to us, "The fact is, my whole family came from Kiev." Then the man asserted—he did not suggest—that they were both Jews. Lou allowed that it might be so. There was a terrible urgency in the manner of the man from Kiev, especially when he stopped as if he had come to the end of what he had to say.

Lou was taken aback by the visit, the claim of kinship, the assertion of a common condition as Jews. He was very much moved by the drama of the stranger's incursion into his hotel room. He was at a loss to know what to do. He was also terribly put out. For a moment he entertained the possibility that it was all a put-up job, designed to embarrass an American visitor politically. But he rejected the notion.

The Rogozhin from Kiev waited urgently.

Lou pointed to his watch. He said and signed that he had a dinner engagement. He had to meet many persons at that dinner. It was very important. He was obliged to attend. After all, he was a guest of the Soviet Union. At the words Soviet Union the other Rogozhin became voluble in his turn. Lou judged that the Soviet Union was precisely the issue.

What was he to do? The man from Kiev was speaking with great emphasis, at great speed. Lou could not make out a word of it. Unfortunately, he was in no doubt at all about what that stream of incomprehensible language meant.

Lou told the other Rogozhin that he had to be at the Gorky Institute at nine o'clock in the morning. At noon — he pointed at his watch — he would be free. He would meet the man from Kiev at the entrance. They would talk at length.

Lou put out his hand. The stranger looked at him. Lou said, "So I'll see you tomorrow. Gorky Institute." The other Rogozhin took Lou's hand, turned, went to the door, and disappeared.

Lou said, "And then I went to that dinner. As it turned out, it was no big deal. I could have missed it."

"Did you see him the next day?"

"I waited an hour, but he never showed."

Diana said, "That's terrible. You'll never have that chance again."

"It's worse than that. I can't get it out of my mind. The hotel lobby was swarming with obvious plainclothes snoops. God knows how he managed to get from Kiev to Moscow in the first place. In that country you don't just pick up and go. You don't just buy a ticket. How had he managed? How had he got as far as my hotel room? What happened when he left my room? I can't get it off my mind."

Diana said that he must write about it. It shouldn't be lost. Lou said that he had been thinking of doing that, for therapy at least. But it seemed cold-blooded to put words together, making reading matter out of what had happened. Diana said, "You can't fix it now. It shouldn't be lost."

"Well, I guess I will do it. But I hate to start."

Some six months later we saw Lou at a party. He looked fine—no more pneumonia. He was relaxed and cheerful. Diana asked if he had written that story. His face changed. But I had felt ashamed of her before that, as soon as I had heard the first words. Lou said that he had made some false starts. The trouble was the impulse to present himself in a softer light. That got in the way each time. He was disgusted with himself. My embarrassment at his being compelled to make an accounting faded a little because the confession was so interesting. Then Diana said something else. "If you're not going to write it, I will." "No, no," Lou said. "I'm going to write it. But it's hard."

I should think so. What was he supposed to write? *Notes from Underground*, perhaps. I don't hold with those ugly self-indictments. Diana says on that point that all the evidence has long been available, the demonstration has long been conclusive. By rights the human experiment should have ended long ago. I know what she means, but what does she propose, mass suicide? Never fear, we're working on it. No ethics, I mean no conduct, grows out of her observation. For example, what do we do with the children? In the meantime, it seems to me, we might as well have good manners as a social emollient. I shrink when she backs the representative man against the wall: "If you won't write it, I will." And isn't there a contradiction here? In the end I think of the ghost in Sartre's machine. Everything is contingent, everything is absurd, there is no point to anything—but you're expected to strive to be "authentic" nonetheless. I suppose that a Frenchman has to keep smuggling honor in, under whatever disguise. But what's Diana's excuse? She's your Yankee crank, hard to live with.

We saw Lou some time after. No, he hadn't written the story. Diana threatened to confiscate it again. Lou said that he really meant to write it, if only because she would stop threatening him when he did.

As near as I can remember we saw Lou again about a year after that. Five minutes for inquiries into the physical and spiritual health of the people we know in common, and Diana did it again. "Have you written that story?"

Lou said, "That business bothered me for a long time. A long time. What I think about it now is that every single Jew in the Soviet Union wants out. It's a terrible problem. But I overreacted. Here's a historical situation, very painful, and I felt that I should have been able to solve it all by myself, and I had failed to do it. That business doesn't bother me anymore. But my reaction to it, it went on and on. That tells me something about my psyche that, frankly, I find embarrassing."

Diana didn't tell him that she would write it herself.

As we were walking home, I said, "How do you like them apples?"

She didn't answer.

"I mean, what he's made out of that incident. It's dead and buried."

"He couldn't bear it anymore." She sounded subdued.

"Couldn't bear what?"

"What he had done. You're annoyed with him now. But, you know, it's not bad character. It's his virtue that made him cancel out what he had done. He couldn't bear it."

Well, I resisted that for five minutes, but in silence. Then, "I suppose that's right."

"Of course it's right."

At that moment I thought, Diana's finished with it. She can't be impersonally judicious about it anymore. She'll never write it now. I'll claim it myself, the way Columbus claimed the New World, all of it, in the name of Isabella the Catholic. Lou can't use it, Diana doesn't need it. Those two Rogozhins—that was the name that came to me as we went along the dark streets—those two Rogozhins loom through history. Those two Rogozhins are the race of man. One is in sore need, the other turns aside. Through the life of man the two take up these roles by turns. Here is a familiar instance, with no cruelty or special malice involved: A man needs a job, he's been out of work for a long time, down on his luck. You don't want to hire him. When I was in a position to hire that man I didn't want to. When a man's been out of work for a long time there may be something wrong with him. Even if it's not his fault he's demonstrated that he's unlucky. You don't want the infection to spread to your enterprise, your department. I've also been the man out of a job for a long time. When you've had senior posts and you leave the job or lose it, nobody wants you, you're damaged goods. And you're not a malleable youngster. You're used to authority and privilege—you say to this one, come, and he comes, and to that one, go, and he goes. What employer in his right mind would want to take you on, with your experience, with your expectation of privilege, with your habit of taking the initiative? I've sat on the other side of the desk, asking for a job, and feeling pity for the man behind it who was twisting and turning, finding me overqualified for his humble little company—once, out of *Schadenfreude* I said, Yes, that's right, I know I am, and that put the other Rogozhin off his stroke. Or wringing his hands because I lacked one area of expertise that in fact he had no use for. I've thought, You poor son of a bitch, why am I distressing you like this? Why am I threatening to loose the plague upon you? And all the while I had to keep my face looking amiable and unconcerned. That is on the most familiar, most anodyne level. The depths are worse. Or so I suspect.

Because that other Rogozhin is my unknown soldier. He does duty for all the betrayals, defections that I don't know I've committed. Or say that like Lou I had to change their coloration in order to go on living in my skin. But worse are the things I am simply not aware of having done, the things I read about in the papers, the things for which I castigate the wretched politicians, the things for which I have a ready panacea. A case like that, I say, it would be cleaner and more manly to put a bullet in him at once and forget the whole business. I say that often. But I have the conviction that it could be said about me.

That may be why I am inclined to forgive the treacheries I have endured myself. Example: Not too long ago now I was lunching with a colleague. The firm we worked for was in trouble, and the two of us had much the same view of the long course of mismanagement that had brought about the trouble. We had been allies. Besides, I liked the man. I said, "I wanted particularly to persuade you that this little-England policy, adopted in panic, is no way to run a company. Of course we have to retrench now. But for the long run, bread and water is the wrong corrective for a business. Our real problem is that we're too small, designedly too small, and we're too vulnerable to a single bad season. In the long run, so that there can be a long run, we simply must expand."

He put down his glass, leaned over the table, and said in a tone I had never heard from him, "What I'm worrying about is how to survive this year."

I understood at once. But I wanted to make sure. That is, I liked the man, I wanted to have misunderstood. So I said,

"We're going to survive the year. But our policy should not be to starve the enterprise. These things are habit-forming."

"What I'm worrying about is how to survive this year—this year, not any other. And I want you to know where I'm coming from."

He was a grown man. He had reached back into the sixties for that expression. The uncharacteristic violence told me that I had heard it right the first time. Later that day, Diana telephoned, and I told her about the lunch. "I'm going to be fired." She said it certainly looked that way.

It took three weeks to happen. When it did, I went to my man's office to say good-bye. He wished me luck. And then, "I have to tell you that I was consulted about it, and I agreed." I said, "Ah." The truth is that I didn't know how to be angry with him. When he was consulted he had seen what the alignment of forces was. Now, that is order-of-battle information, and he would have been a fool to ignore it. He had joined the stronger side. But because of his virtue, as Diana might have said, he had to be angry with me. Probably he felt that I had put him in an exposed position, something one could reasonably be angry about. And then he was angry because he had to cast his vote against me. Everything considered, that is a kind of virtue. Especially since, only two weeks before the day on which he had wanted me to know where he was coming from, he had complained to another colleague—complained and commiserated as people do when they know their company is in trouble — and what he had said got back to me within the hour. His complaint was that those at the top had nothing good to say about me. And he said, "Just who do they think doubled this company's net worth in two years' time?" Interesting. But thinking about all that, I've never been more than surprised. Well, possibly a little disappointed.

You have to get used to these things early. I was twenty-eight when I was drafted into the Army. In my training regiment the average age was about eighteen. In January I fell down on the march and I found myself in the pneumonia ward with eighteen-year-olds. While the kids had fever their flesh fell away. When the fever abated they felt as if they were starving. They heard that there was going to be a grand inspection and they named me spokesman for the collective stomach. The day came, a general appeared, the boys who could not stand were supported at attention by the ones who could, and we were inspected, the quick and the dead. The general knew the drill. He asked a boy about the food at once. It was fine. The general was conscientious, and he asked another boy the same thing. The food was fine. He was a step away from me, and then he was facing me. I wished that I were in uniform and booted rather than in a bathrobe and slippers. Anyway, I broke the law. "Sir, the men have asked me to speak for them. They're young and they're hungry." The general looked at me with distaste, but he said, "Men, don't you get seconds?" There was no answer. The nurse who was the nutritionist said, "Sir, the men get seconds. And thirds if they want them." I said, "Sir, no man in this ward has seen seconds. The food trays come and then they're taken away."

The general said, "Sergeant."

"Sir!"

"The messes are to be inspected regularly, with particular attention to the adequacy of the ration. These men are soldiers. They must be made fit for duty as soon as possible."

The general and his party left. The boys sagged onto their cots. I was still standing, in bathrobe and slippers, blind with rage. I ranted at them for cowards—forgetting that they were children—and to drive the lesson home every second word was ugly. I was getting a good deal of satisfaction out of the silent attention being accorded me. Then I turned and saw that a party of nurses at the far end of the ward was listening, rapt, to my eloquence. You have to be forgiving, else you play the fool. You say, all men are corrupt, Rogozhin is a man, ergo Rogozhin is more corrupt than any.

Here is another story I heard, or dreamed. It takes place during the Second World War. A young man was third officer of a freighter in a large convoy in the Irish Sea. The freighter was armed with a three-inch fifty at the stern and three 20-millimeter antiaircraft Oerlikon guns mounted in steel and concrete tubs on pedestals rising from the decks, one in the bows of the ship and the other two on either side of the bridge. It was early days, and there were no Navy gun crews to serve the guns; the seamen stood their regular sea watches and then the gun watches. During the Atlantic crossing one man in the deck crew had fallen asleep while on bow lookout, a second time while on lookout on the wing of the bridge, and a third time last night in the forward gun tub. Just before dawn the vessel took a torpedo in the number-two hold and in a very short time she was down by the head. The whistle sounded abandon ship. It was blowing nearly a whole gale, but all four boats were lowered and manned without incident. The young third mate was in command of his double-banked boat, standing up in the stern sheets at the long steering oar, heading to windward to escape the burning oil from a torpedoed tanker. The oil flamed on the backs of the high swell and the crests of an ugly cross-sea. The men pulled steadily, making little way over the ground but drawing away from the sinking ship drifting to leeward and from the body of the convoy that steamed on to the north.

What with the sound of wind and water, a shout would scarcely carry to the bows of the boat. The mate leaned down as far as he could while tending the steering oar, and cried to the stroke that in a few minutes they would stop pulling, stream the sea anchor, whack out the dry rations—hardtack, canned pemmican, cigarettes—and wait to be picked up by the British navy. "Pass it on." The stroke feathered his oar, turned to his mate on the rowing bench, spoke to him, and both men turned to call to the men just forward of them. The officer watched those gestures travel forward in the twisting, pitching boat till it reached the men at the bow oars. He was on the point of calling out, "Give way," when he saw the same gestures coming back towards him. He bent again to the stroke, who said, "Dacy won't eat the hardtack. He worked in the factory."

The mate looked up towards the man who pulled the port oar at the bow, who had twice fallen asleep on lookout and last night during his gun watch. He said to the stroke oar, "Dacy will eat his hardtack with the rest of us. Pass it on." The boat had lost steerageway as soon as the men had stopped pulling, and the steering oar was less effective and harder to manage. The mate was impatient to see the word reach the man in the bow. As soon as it had he cried, "Give way together." The men forward could not hear, but they saw the stroke and his partner bend to take a short starting pull.

At that moment the man in the bow stood up, letting go his oar—his partner on the bench seized it before it slipped overboard. The man began to clamber aft between the pair on the next rowing thwart. As he did an unusually high sea lifted the bow; he fell upon both the rowers as they pulled. They said something to him. Then the sea ran the length of the boat, and he righted himself and moved aft to the next thwart. The mate saw another sea, higher still, approaching swiftly, terrifying with its uplifted weight of water. He thought, When it lifts her bow she'll pitchpole. The rowing men and the man coming towards him could not see the great wave running at their backs. Now the man coming aft was on the thwart forward of the stroke oars, and he was just setting a foot into the well behind their bench. The mate thought, If she doesn't pitchpole she'll slew to one side and swamp, unless I can keep the oar bearing. He stepped quickly to starboard over the loom of the steering oar and grasped the handle with his left hand. The man coming towards him had a knee on the aftermost thwart now, between the stroke oars. The oarsmen were at the end of their pull, starting to bend forward and recover. The mate stooped as the wave lifted the bow of the boat. He snatched the oak stretcher from under the feet of the two oarsmen before him, raised it, brought it down on the head of the kneeling man whose arms reached out to him. The boat reared on the swell so that it seemed almost to be standing on end. The mate dropped the stretcher and in the same motion thrust his right hand into the armpit of the man now falling athwart the gunwale and with a lifting shove sent him overboard. The stern slewed suddenly, but with both hands on the steering oar and throwing all his weight against it the mate checked the swing. The wave was well under the boat, now nearly on an even keel, and then the bow dipped dizzily into the trough. The man overboard was hidden from the oarsmen by the bulk of the running wave. Even after it had traveled some distance they could not find him for the other seas that sank and towered.

A good many years now, off and on, I have thought about that. The incident might be disposed of but for an odd detail. That is, the man Dacy had made love to his fate. Surely a struggle in the stern sheets of a boat in a gale is intolerable. There was, however, the odd detail. It appears that in abandoning ship the officer had slipped a revolver into his waistband. It was under his buttoned peacoat. He had not thought to show the pistol to the mutineer, and later he was troubled by that omission—he had deprived Dacy of a last chance to live. And yet an enraged man is not always pacified by the sight of a revolver, and this man had shown clear signs of derangement. Were there world enough and time, surely it would be everyone's duty to protect and comfort a man so afflicted. But a ship's boat under stress of weather is little room and every instant is a danger. When you have presented a pistol and there is no good effect you must pull the trigger, and in a reeling boat planted thick with men it would be easy to strike an innocent, easier still to hole the boat. No, I have long ago absolved the young officer unused to carrying a weapon who forgot that he had one under his coat. It troubles the mind's eye, but I think it very good fortune that he forgot.

So, while the pistol presents itself to conscience even after many years, that murdered man cannot do duty as my

Rogozhin. And I have forgotten or never known the man who might. I have to choose the available candidate. I see very well that my friend Lou cannot use his Rogozhin. Diana, as far as I can tell, does not require one — someone inspired once exclaimed that she must be in this generation that one just man for whose sake God withholds his hand from destroying the race. Whom they abandon I must grapple to me. My comrade, my companion in the dark.

A PARENTHESIS

When I was setting out on my travels during the war my father told me, "Never provoke a man to a fight. Never raise your hands to a man. If he falls and his head strikes the ground you might be responsible for his death."

This in the context of a world war. But at a hundred and forty pounds soaking wet the policy made sense to me. I thought I could keep it in mind. Then my father said, "There are times when you see a fight coming and you can't get out of it. In that case don't hesitate. Be sure you strike the first blow while your man is working himself up to it. With luck that may end the business. At very least you've caught him off balance. Don't wait. It's too dangerous."

Since I was a pure young lad with no experience of life I thought that my father's views were paradoxical. Look before you leap; he who hesitates is lost. He was an old soldier, but I discounted his experience even as I was taking in his advice with ingrained filial piety. What he discounted was my temperament. I could hardly bear the idea of striking first—as an idea. And there are other ways of provoking a man besides showing him a fist. No doubt my father knew all that and was just doing what he could for me.

A couple of years later I was in New Orleans, in uniform, in a draft of men who had orders for the southwest Pacific. The first step was to board a troop train for San Francisco. I nearly missed making that first step. The day before we were to leave we were all given six injections—six needles, the medics called them. I hoped those needles might keep me safe from bush fever, blackwater fever, cholera, malaria, and drowning. But when the alarm clock went off the next morning, and I jumped out of bed in concert with my three bunkmates, I found myself on the floor and could not pick myself up. I must have looked odd. My friends lifted me onto the bed, and when they had washed and dressed they cleaned me up a bit and dressed me. They took my duffel downstairs. When the taxi pulled up they carried me down and hauled me into it. At the railroad station they bore me along to the platform, enthroned me on our four seabags, hunted up a handtruck, and told me to guard it with my fading life. Then they went off to collect the day's rumors.

The handtruck was upright beside me. I held on to one of the crossbars to help me sit up straight. My stomach was aflutter, the contents of my skull felt like tapioca before it sets, I had broken into a sweat. Then a boy came along with his seabag on his shoulder. I knew him by sight. "Let me have the handtruck. I've got a lot of gear to move." I told him that I couldn't do that, it had been left in my charge. He started to turn away but his eyes were still on me. He said, "You son of a bitch."

At once I was on my feet. He dropped his bag and took a step towards me. I was taking a step towards him, and when we had closed the distance I hit him and he fell. He was still for a moment, thinking things over. Then he gathered his limbs, got to his feet, swung his bag to his shoulder, and went off.

I was astonished at the automatism of the impulse that had raised me from my seat. My head was clear, I felt quite fit. A moment ago I could not have imagined that I would be able to stand without help. I was not interested in anything else. Certainly I felt no scruple at having struck the first blow—it had come to me by inspiration. Above all I marveled that adrenaline could suffuse the body in an instant, rousing the animal spirits. Or that was a sample of my notions of physiology as those things were understood in my youth, ranking perhaps with the principle of phlogiston and the theory of the humors. My friends came up, surprised to find me standing. I told them how I defended the handtruck. They were puzzled but not otherwise impressed.

The train was eight days crossing America to San Francisco. On the second or third day one of my friends noticed that the boy I had knocked down was missing a front tooth.

"What did you want to do that for?" I didn't care for his tone. Hadn't they charged me to hold on to that handtruck? Hadn't the other fellow called me a son of a bitch? Then I ran into him. It was surprising that it had not happened sooner, for the men of the draft paraded through the dining car with their mess kits for breakfast, lunch, and supper. That young fellow had a particularly pleasant face, and now there was a gap in it. I ran into him again and again afterwards. We did not speak, but he looked at me as if he felt no animosity. We had been intimate on that station platform, and now that the excitement was over he did not care to discuss it — that was all. As the days passed, my sense of my own merit, usually strong, began to flag because of the breach I had made behind his upper lip.

It did not go beyond that. My gift for introspection is small. Only after many years I see its connection with other things that have happened to me, some that I remember with pained clarity and beyond those a penumbra of misgiving. Let me say what I would be getting at. In a matter of this kind, perhaps only a man whose life is opaque to him could find his way to an insight of the kind. He has such difficulty in seeing the pattern of his actions that the subject is never at rest. He has gone through life shaking his head over it. And now things come together of themselves to make something resembling what the academy — though not on occasions like mine — calls a contribution to knowledge.

When I was a child, somewhere between six and seven,

my father bought me a handsome bow. He told me that it was made of lemonwood. Long afterwards, when I read that the Indians of the South made their bows of Osage orange, I remembered my bow, which could claim a kind of kinship with those, if only for the names. The grip was wrapped about with green cloth that had a nap to it, so that your hand would not slip. My father pointed out that the bowstring of Irish linen had an eye-splice at either end, and he showed me how to brace the bow by stepping inside it, using my leg as well as my arms to bend it, and to slide the string along the upper limb to the groove at its tip. The arrows too were enchanting, each with its cock feather. He showed me how to nock the arrow to the bowstring, always at the same place. He put a few turns of cotton thread on the string, just above and just below the place, to remind me of it until I could find it by habit. He showed me how to draw the nocked arrow all the way back to my cheekbone, and how to release the string. He was romantic. He told me that when I had learned to shoot properly, at full draw I would feel that all my body was "inside the bow." I never reached that stage, but I remember the pleasure he took in telling me that bit of bowcraft, real or nostalgic. And I have since heard horn players say that sometimes the horn will sound a note that is beyond what the musician's craft can compass. The horn knows that the player can do no more, and out of sympathy and professional pride utters the note for him.

The next day my father took me to the park, and I carried

my bow, which I had slept with. He used to pay great attention to lighting his cigar. He smoked for the pleasure of it, he was calm and temperate, and he always did his part so that the cigar would burn evenly, draw sweetly. When I was older and had learned how to enjoy his enjoyment, I used to ask him, once his cigar was properly lit, how it seemed. He would smile and say, "Good." Or he would say, "This cigar holds its ash well, but it has no character." Any report delighted me. On that day, however, I was much too young to play with him in that way. I was simply aware that he was lighting his cigar, and I went on a little in advance of him, loosing arrows over the grassy field.

The wonder of flight! To send the arrow far, again and again. At some point in this engrossing game a small boy whom I had not seen darted past me and pounced upon the arrow where it had fallen. I shouted, "Hey!" He turned with the arrow in his hand and I snatched it from him. As I did that I saw that his face was alight, but in a moment it changed. I do not remember how the boy was removed from my view. It was as if I could see only straight before me, my eyes fixed on the hateful deed. My father's disappointment and chagrin—"That little boy meant to give it to you!"—added nothing to my discovering, in my own will, the boundless faithlessness of the world.

In my will? The cry had welled up in me from artesian sources, I had been helpless in the matter. Lifelong, I have apologized to all the world, rarely to my neighbor, scarcely ever for the right reason. Naturally I have not gone unassisted by others in this career. I did not have a special talent for it. And I don't complain that circumstances have been against me in one case or another. I prefer to be angry instead. My saving formula is that I am good-natured but bad-tempered. If someone were to point out the flaw in this portrait I would simply shrug. It's the best I can come up with, and it does me little good. I do know that the world is hospitable to life — our presence here is the proof. Then, I have met with generosity everywhere, starting with the man who said to me when I was sixteen, speaking in a low tone so as not to give the show away, "Here, kid. Watch what I do. Brace your knee against your wrist when you push the shovel handle. And when you throw the shovelful, give it a flirt — like this — so's the dirt falls in one heap where you want it." In danger, people have saved me from harm without giving it a thought because that is what people do. I hope they are not burdened with a character like mine. It is my fear that they may be, because I too have met danger for the sake of others without a thought. And in louche situations people have gone bail for me morally, reminding me that I am not without honor — since the man suspected despairs of himself. But for all that, one mustn't fail to recognize the limits of an idea. The cordial impulse, the generous self-forgetting is not the only habit of the race. On a hot summer's day when I was ten years old and the city seemed deserted, an older boy from another neighborhood came upon me and boxed my ears for something to do. We were on a long hill. He was above me, I below, and when I saw what he was at I kept my hands up and blocked his punches at my head, which was the most convenient part of me for him to hit because he was taller and uphill. When your arms have been upraised for five minutes they are heavy, particularly if you have to work with them. I was most afraid of a black eye that would mean Hail, Columbia when I went home—Mother ran a tight ship, skipper next to God. Then the boy noticed that he was not landing many blows, and he had a clever thought. I say clever because in these cases to break the rhythm of your movements is very difficult—think how trained fencers often cannot break off the obsessive rhythm of the *tac au tac* but carry it on like machines—and that boy had an idea and the discipline to stop what he was doing. He walked around me and settled himself comfortably downhill. Now he could feint at my head and strike for real anywhere on the left side of my chest. Both of us were shirtless. Busy as I was I divined that my chest was taking bruises that would soon be black and blue. The social consequences I had in mind were much more serious than the bruises. But the drubbing must have gone on for a good ten minutes more, with me retreating uphill in relative good order over some hundred and fifty yards. At the point when I felt too weary to keep my hands up any longer that boy gave me his back and strolled away. Perhaps his hand was hurting from the repeated blows upon my bony chest. At last I made my way home, walking a little lopsidedly. Mother saw at once that I had been fighting. She said, "Just wait till your father comes home," and she gave me a licking. Well, that is a manner of speaking. She slapped my face just once, one of those roundhouse slaps that burn the cheek, bring water to your eye, and resound inside your sconce. Justice is almost always more painful than crime.

One mustn't dwell on these matters. Thanked be fortune it hath been otherwise, twenty times better. On *The City of Biloxi*, when I was eighteen and an able seaman, we had the testimony of two young men about the married state. Harry and Frank came from Chicago. Both were married. They were going to sea because it was wartime; they were friends and shipped together. Though they were in the black gang, we aristocrats of the deck crew set aside class distinctions and courted their company; they were that decent. O'Brien, the ordinary seaman in our watch, a Texan and cynic maybe sixteen years old, had startled us once when he called out to a bumboatman who had come alongside where we swung at anchor off Viña del Mar to swap Spanish brandy—Fundador—for American cigarettes, *¿A que hora se cierran las tiendas?* He had been keeping his Mexican mother to himself because he was sensitive. O'Brien who, when we were taking down the spar deck at sea—steel stanchions, I-beams eight feet high, steel crossbeams upon them supporting rough timbers—and with the bolts removed we were throwing the steel overboard to sink and the timbers to float (dangers to navigation), O'Brien had one end of a timber, I the other, each sidling along on his steel beam with nothing between us but air and the timber, and I called to him, "Hold it!" because I had to change my grip, and he waited perhaps two seconds, then threw his end away. The timber very nearly took me overboard with it. I had to push it away hard to keep my perch on the beam. O'Brien was already marching in the other direction. I had my sheath knife on my belt and I was afraid to look at him, afraid to hear his voice. I went below to the fo'c's'le and sat down on my bunk. The bosun came after me. "What are you doing below?" I told him that if I went on deck I'd kill that Mexican mick. "You're not going to kill anybody. Put that knife in your locker for now. He's just a green kid. You're a seaman—grumble you may but go you must. On deck." I felt much relieved at being ordered about. But when I went on deck I told my particular friend of it—he was the other AB in our watch. "Why do you want to kill him? He's not very big and he has freckles." I told my friend that he wasn't getting the point. "No, no. I saw it all. I saw you dancing on the spar deck. I told O'Brien that when two men lift together they drop the load together. I told him he nearly sent you overboard. You know what he said to that? 'I wouldn't miss him.' " And my friend laughed and laughed.

O'Brien, then, when we were anchored in the roadstead

off Antofagasta, with its barren red mountain and the great blaze of white that said "*Gloria a O'Higgins,*" O'Brien put a question to Harry: "What's it like to make love with the same woman all the time? Don't you get sick and tired?" Harry considered him. At last, "Are you talking smut, or is that a serious question?" Naturally O'Brien had to protest that it was a serious question. "The way it is," Harry said, "is that when you love a woman and you live with her you love her more and more. Isn't that right, Frank?" Frank said, "That's right." There was a silence. We had something to think about. Including O'Brien, I imagine, who had long ago thought of everything and must have heard another side of the story. That Harry was generous, like a *vin généreux.* He thought it was his business to offer the world to his juniors.

A few months earlier I had been on a tanker in the North Atlantic. One night in heavy weather, with the ship taking green seas on deck, I had to stand my bow lookout on the wing of the bridge, where instead of the danger of being washed overboard I endured the freezing wind. When I was relieved by the other AB in the watch I was numb with the noise of the gale as much as with the cold. I clambered slowly down the bridge ladder become an enemy in the reeling, leaping ship, and I opened and dogged shut behind me the watertight door. It was almost quiet in the gangway, except when the stern of the vessel lifted, the screw was half out of the water and raced and pounded, and the steel plates of the hull vibrated, groaned, and screeched. It was warm in the gangway. I turned into the mess to get some coffee from the big urn. A man from the black gang was lodged in a corner behind the mess table, trying to find the right chord on his guitar. A voice made a quiet suggestion. The man with the guitar said, "Can you play this thing?" I had just filled my mug and I looked up. The guitar was changing hands. "A little." The last speaker was the watertender. He had just come from his watch in the engine room and he wore no shirt. First he tuned the guitar to his satisfaction, putting his ear down to it when the screw raced. Then he chocked himself between the table and the bulkhead, and he strummed a little. After a moment be began to sing in a light voice.

> There's a mist upon the Rio Colorado,
> There's a haze upon the western Texas moon.
> Someone waits for me across the Colorado.
> Someone hopes that I'll be back in Texas soon.

He did not look up. He watched the fingers of his left hand and sang diffidently so that the song seemed incidental. There was no mistaking it for anything but one of the dirges of the American spirit, the twang of commingled longing and defeat. I was struck by the verse, unemphatic as the singing. It spoke of "someone" in the largest terms, in a frame of water, earth, and sky. And "someone" was not named because the song was shy about love.

He sang the second verse, letting it trail off softly. He passed the guitar back to his mate, who told him to give us another. But he said, "No. Here you go. I have to get some sleep." I think of him, just come from the heat and racket of the engine room, his skin as red as if he had been in a sauna, his bent left arm with its boss of muscle, his fingers sliding along the neck of the guitar. What a piece of work is man. He had been wiper—lowly as an ordinary seaman—then oiler, then watertender, watching his gauges for hours at a stretch. I would like to think that he got to be third engineer, for he was studying for the rate, then second, then chief. In those wartime days the casualties in merchant ships were 25 percent, which delighted my father and made for swift promotion. I hope he was not drowned in the war.

A WHILE back I hinted darkly at a revelation. What on earth did I have in mind? It seems that I am simply not educable. I can't learn. Years and years ago I saw what should have been for me a conclusive demonstration, carried out by just such an oaf as myself. After the war when I was a college freshman it happened that I was late in registering for my classes because ships do not always reach their port at the scheduled time. I was a week overdue when I showed up for my first class. The room was full of students. There was one unoccupied seat at the end of the last row. "Always room for another victim," the fellow nearest me said. I sat down, prepared to listen to the lecture. But I did look at my neighbor and the other students in the row. I saw at once that they were ball players. There was no mistaking their hefty frames, large limbs, and lounging air; half the football team was represented in that row. The professor was discussing what he called the dynamics of literature. His remarks seemed abstract, but I found them interesting because it had never occurred to me that one could systematize poems, plays, novels, and stories, reducing them to a seemly order of types, of styles, of intentions, of effects, of motifs — as it were, a general grammar of art. And discoursing in that way he made a philosophical observation. He suggested that the literary arts aspire to be co-extensive with the gamut of human joy and sorrow — that was the way he put it. I thought the idea was splendid. And then he brought drama to the classroom. Extending his left arm eastward in Eden, he said, "Comedy." And paused. Then he stretched out his right arm westward in an elegant Delsarte gesture: "Tragedy." The class took it in without blinking, but not the jocks in the back row. You've seen pigeons waddling about, pecking in the public square, and a truck goes by and backfires with the sound of a heavy-caliber gun, and every pigeon rises and wheels in panic and perfect alignment. That was how the back row ducked down to hide its uncontainable mirth. Red-faced and shaking they saluted the learned idiocy. It takes good reflexes to play ball, and athletes of that sort work on Napoleon's principle that first you engage the enemy and then you find out what his dispositions are. Is there any other way to live one's life? For a moment I understood how much active intelligence it took to play ball. Naturally, the general prejudice against inspiration gracefully chronic overwhelmed me once more like a breaking sea. But for a privileged instant the ball players had shown me what it means to address an issue while looking at how good you are looking, playing the fool.

Let me try it again. This is what happened.

The troopship made a landfall in New Guinea and our draft of seamen was set ashore. It was late afternoon. In a little while a dozen Australian sailors joined us, having come from God knows where. Our own men were all a little light-headed, I think, breathing in the odors of the land that we had first scented during the previous night, perhaps a hundred miles out to sea. The Australians rolled and smoked their strong tobacco, the Americans lit their tailor-mades, and still the spice of the massed vegetation beyond the fringe of coco palms on the beach made us uneasy with every breath we drew. The sun went down. We were mustered around a kerosene lantern, and names were called from a list. The first name was that of a man I had remarked on the trooper. We were all pretty well tanned, at least above the waist, because there was little shade on the ship's deck, and the hold, fitted out with bunks on three levels, was simply unbearable during the day. Under our tan was the curious jaundice-yellow of Atabrine, the drug we had to swallow every day against malaria, with the pharmacist's mate seeing to it, checking off each name on the roster. But that man was tanned to the color of cordovan leather, and the yellow dye showing through the maroon of his skin was eerie. There were other oddities about him. He was tall, his chin was always above the horizontal, as if he was prepared to look down on whatever you might tell him, and his chest was flat for a man who was often called upon to do heavy work out in the weather. His shoulders were drawn far back as if they were seized with cramp, and lifted very high, so that his neck and throat appeared to have sunk an inch or more into his chest. Looking at him full face there was nothing to trouble you, if you had not yet come to associate his features with his swagger and his braying assurance. But once, when I came on deck through the companionway, from darkness into brilliant light, I saw him in profile twenty feet off. He was grinning, with all his teeth exposed on the one side of his face that I could see. I was startled, as if I had heard an unexpected gunshot nearby or the crash of two vehicles colliding in the street. My shoulders went up in a sudden spasm, my neck sank into my chest. That man dismayed me.

Now, I am not usually timorous or apprehensive. I am generally good in emergencies, since I lack the imagination of disaster. In a ruckus of any kind I am more likely to be savage than frightened. What? They're picking on my mother's little boy again? But I was afraid of that man. His face in profile, grinning, reminded me of an animal's jaws and snout. I was so taken aback that I could not put a name to the animal. The sea was calm, but as if we were in heavy weather I scuttered across the deck to the port bulwark, as far as I could get from him. It took me some time to recover. I looked mechanically at the vessels keeping station in the convoy, taking their maneuvers from the hospital ship that bore the commodore. Mechanically I looked astern for the *Botha*, an old coal-burner, an eight-knot ship that fell behind whenever there was a blow, as had happened in the night. That vessel was invisible under the horizon, but I made out the smudge of her smoke. When I had satisfied myself about the *Botha*'s whereabouts I found that a line of the Christmas carol was running in my head. *Caput apri defero.* His snout and his tusked jaws were those of a boar.

The next name called belonged to that man's sidekick, a short, silent fellow who was always with him. Clearly, there were people who did not fear and detest the cordovan man. My shipmate, the one who had decreed that I spare O'Brien's life, didn't seem to mind him at all—he was on this voyage too. But I excused him because he was very brave. He had no head for heights, yet he went up the mast like everyone else, except that he had to do it in a cold sweat. That takes courage. You could say with the French, the craft requires it. Well, yes. But it takes courage. Besides, he was never one to be at war with mankind.

They brought up a number of weapons carriers fitted out with benches. In the gleam of the headlights we climbed aboard with our gear. My friend was on the bench opposite mine, looking about curiously. I looked to the right as a man, the cordovan man, pitched down beside me, and quickly I looked away. We rode for perhaps half an hour on a rough track to the beach at Buna where the battle had taken place. The headlights showed that nearly every palm tree had been docked by shellfire at a height of ten feet or so. An Englishman seated at a table under a lantern in a large, open tent greeted us in a loud voice. Again we heard our names, and as he called them out he assigned tent numbers to the men, two by two. To my horror he paired me with Morgan, the cordovan man. We turned to look at each other. In a voice louder than necessary, as if I had taken the Englishman's cue, I said I would rather bunk with a friend, and I named him. The cordovan man said he felt the same way. The Englishman said, "As you please, gentlemen. I'm interested only in having you all billeted. Do tell me if you have a preference."

We were idle for perhaps ten days. Naturally we got acquainted with the Australian seamen. Their outlook was much like that of a number of Israelis whom I came to know later in life; they were pioneers verging on freebooters. The Aussies would say by way of commendation, "He's a scrounger," meaning that the man in question went far beyond the sailor's penchant for picking up without authorization whatever might possibly turn out to be useful. I gathered that a good scrounger was a man who knew how to live. I found the Aussies livelier and more curious than my countrymen. In part it was because they labored under a grievance. They felt their nationality as a predicament, and they looked for opportunities to defend their predicament. In the year that I spent among them I saw it demonstrated often. An Australian would find a fresh American, someone with whom he could renew the quarrel. The Aussie would say, "Just how big do you think Australia is?" Usually the American declined to guess or to care. "About the size of Rhode Island you think, eh?" The American would shrug. "Maybe half as big as Texas, eh? Well, it's more than two-thirds of the entire extent of the United bloody States, and put that in your pipe." Beyond their fervent national claims they seemed to me to have rather more character than our bunch, ranging from eccentricity to forceful temperament, as if their instinct made them give rein to their individual bent, were it ever so crooked. I had imagined that the Americans, raised in God's country, were diverse and picturesque enough. But the Yanks did not show up that well; I knew that by introspection.

At the end of the ten days my friend was assigned a berth as mate on a bald-headed schooner. I did not know what contribution to the war effort a vessel of that kind could make, but I was jealous of his shipping in sail and ready to feel lonely. Two or three days later a score of us were ordered aboard a small coaster for Milne Bay, a day and a night's passage. The rainy season had just begun. Our quarters were so cramped that we had to stow our seabags on deck, and the gear was wet through with rain and salt spray. We sailed into the long strait of Milne Bay that ended in a munitions dump, and found there a larger, more cosmopolitan population. A fellow from Lancaster, Pennsylvania, had set up shop as a jeweler in his tent. His specialty was scavenging aluminum from downed aircraft, to be turned into wristwatch bands. He had had the presence of mind to bring his mallet and jeweler's anvil all the way from Lancaster to New Guinea. He explained that in this tropical climate a leather band would mildew and rot in jigtime; it was just common sense to commission an aluminum band from him. And there was a brisk trade in arms. I bought from a soldier a .30 '06 Springfield rifle in new condition, probably issued to a sniper since the graceless Garand had made that fine weapon obsolete for any other purpose. Thirty bucks, which was very high, but the alternative was gambling the money away and I disliked gambling. Another fellow had somehow provided himself with the new Johnson, of which I had never heard. The barrel of the rifle was jacketed with a metal tube pierced all over with holes and shining like chrome. Of course it was chambered for the same ammunition as the old Springfield and the Garand, and that led to an odd happening in the camp.

People gathered around the man with the Johnson rifle. "What's the tube for?" The owner guessed it was to keep you from burning your hand when the barrel was hot, just as most military rifles were sheathed with wood, often all the way to the muzzle. Was it powerful? Just as powerful as the Garand, the owner suggested, since it took the same cartridge.

"I'll tell you one thing. There isn't a cartridge made that'll drive a bullet through a jerrycan full of water." That announcement came from Morgan, the cordovan man. He had come up behind me. I thought that what he had said was an attempt at a joke. Someone asked, "Is that really so?"

"Sure as shootin'."

It seemed so ridiculous that I turned around and asked, "Do you mean the GI jerrycans, the steel ones with a composition lining? Or the tin cans like that one?" I pointed to a five-gallon can just inside the tent of the man with the Johnson rifle.

"Makes no difference. Water is incompressible."

Well, I had heard that somewhere myself and I had taken it on faith. Indeed, I supposed that hydraulic machines were based on that very principle. So I was confused for a moment. Then I remembered that submerged submarines moved through the incompressible water, and fired torpedoes through it too. I said that a bullet from the Johnson would make a small hole in the front of the can and blow a big one out of the back.

The cordovan man was prompt. "Five bucks says you're a liar."

Someone made the suggestion that we try it out. I said

that was fine with me, but the bullet would go right through the can and keep on moving. If we were going to try it we would have to do that where nobody would get killed.

"Ballistics expert chickens out," Morgan said.

Some fifty yards from where we stood, the clearing in which the camp had been set up came to an end. One man shouldered the can, which was nearly full, and we walked towards a grove of bamboo where the land rose steeply. On the theory that no one would be in that grove, the can was placed before it. The man with the Johnson looked at me, a little apprehensive. "Will that thing ricochet?" I said, "Not till it hits a rock. It certainly won't ricochet off a tin can." He lay down, and after fussing with the rifle for a moment, he let off a shot. The can jumped three feet. We walked over to it. The front panel was intact except for a neat hole through its center. The opposite side was deformed, and there was a great rent in it.

"You owe me five bucks," I said to the cordovan man, reaching out my hand.

"Kid, I'd rather owe it to you than beat you out of it."

"Kid, is it?"

"Yes, mother's little lambkin. And don't look at me with those goo-goo eyes. Makes me want to bust out crying."

I didn't know what to say to that. I went on looking at him because he was no longer a ghoul. He had been reduced to a problem, and in a small way to an enemy. After a few moments he saw no point in paying any further attention to me. He turned away, master of all he surveyed.

A PARENTHESIS

Some time later, walking through the camp in the night, I came upon a tent with its walls rolled up overhead, lit by a lantern hanging from the peak, and I heard the now familiar words, "New spinner coming in. Come in, new spinner." The men in the tent were playing crown and anchor, the sailor's roulette. There was no wheel of fortune. Instead there was an oblong panel of green felt upon a rough table, and a grille was drawn upon the felt in white paint, with the necessary cabalistic symbols. The bank cried again, "Come in, new spinner," so as not to break the rhythm of the play. I went in among the crowd, and I saw Morgan shaking the dice in his palm. He won, and a man beside him stepped back and resigned. He won a second time, and another man counted himself out. I took his place, directly across the table from Morgan. He won again, but this time no one moved. He won a fourth time and crowed. He looked around the table. "Everybody sinking fast. Not much starch in this bunch." And he set down his stakes again. I put my money on his, certain that his luck was out. He rolled the dice and lost. I picked up the pot and he stepped back from the table to reorganize. "You don't have a bet, sonny boy." There was more money on the edge of the table before him, and a five-dollar bill showed on the top of the heap. "The hell you say." I snatched up the fiver. "Here's the five you don't owe me for the bet I didn't have with you last time." And I stuffed all the money into the pocket of my dungarees. He hesitated for a moment. Perhaps he decided that what had happened was too public to challenge, for he left the tent. And someone I had not noticed, the fellow who was the cordovan man's buddy, detached himself from the knot of men and followed him.

The play had been disrupted. By rights I was the new spinner, but I never thought of going on. People were lingering uncertainly because there was the sense of unfinished business in the air. After a while they took up my case.

An Australian said, "You're in trouble now." I didn't understand. Another Aussie said, "Morgan's a bad man to cross." Seeing me looking blank, he said, "He's a rough customer. He's a boxer, you know. You don't want to anger a man of that sort."

"Boxer?" I was astonished that anyone could believe that. "Did he say so? Don't you see how he carries his shoulders? He can't hit. I was raised among boxers. I'll take my chances with him anytime."

Instantly I had to regret that. The cordovan man had come by again, just beyond the circle of lantern light, and as I was saying those last words I caught sight of him turning away.

I was too callow to have held my tongue, taken by surprise by the preposterous suggestion. But I was not too young to understand that driving a man into a corner was cruel folly. There was no way for him to retreat. There was no way for him to defend the character he had assumed. I had injured him, turning a loudmouth into a victim. It could not be repaired now. And he would be implacable.

Besides, he was not alone. Two men could always subdue one, even without weapons. I left the tent, not apprehensive for the darkness since no man was going to bushwhack me that night, but troubled about the time to come. I couldn't carry that Springfield wherever I went. That was socially impossible. In any case, if two men mean to waylay you a rifle is no answer at all. I was thinking that I must keep within the camp, not walk about the beach, beautiful in its great green defile, the opposite shore a half-mile away, and when the sun shone the restless blue water between lifting your heart. I must not walk in the bamboo groves. I was a fool.

The next morning was clear and brisk, with a few high clouds, belying the rainy season. I decided to write a letter home. Framing a letter was hard work because of the censorship. I could not say where I was or where I had been, what I was doing or had been doing. No meteorological discussion, please. I wondered why the authorities allowed you to put a date on a letter, since that might be as important a breach of secrecy as the things formally prohibited.

For writing there was a communal picnic table handy, of a sort that has a fixed bench on either side. When I sat down with pen and paper there was a coco palm two feet to my left; the bench had been put right against the trunk of the tree, presumably for its shade. Someone had gone to the trouble of stepping up on the bench with a line, taking a hitch around the trunk at a spot overhead. He had led the line to another palm about twenty feet away. The rolling hitches showed that a seaman had done it. And what other body of men always expects to wash its own clothes? The hitch on the second tree was also higher than a man's head, but the one at the table was higher still by the height of the bench. Any line made fast at both ends takes a catenary curve, no matter how taut you draw it. Cunning as any housewife, the man who had thrown the hitches had calculated the effect of a line's length of wet clothes and done what he could to keep them from trailing on the sodden earth. I sat down at the table and wrote the date.

While I was waiting for inspiration a man came up with a seabag full of laundry. He had washed the bag too; the ensemble dripped as he came along. He set it down on the bench opposite mine. I said, "Good morning."

His answer was, "So you're the boxer."

"I didn't say that. I said something else." Then I was sorry that my tone had been ungracious. I thought I must be rattled still about last night's business. I had never spoken to this chap, an Australian, but he had a pleasant air about him. He did not seem put out by my answer. He began to loosen the hitch at the mouth of his seabag. "The manly art of self-defense," he said with a quiet laugh.

"I'm not a boxer. But I can tell one when I see him."

"Boxing isn't in it, you know. It's a game, boxing. Mug's game. What you want if you have to defend yourself is jiujitsu training. While your boxer is demonstrating his straight left and his right cross he can be put hors de combat by a man who knows his jiujitsu. It's as if you chose to use a fencing foil against an express rifle. Daft, that is."

Here he started to take the wet things out of his seabag. But the topic held him. He went on.

"Jiujitsu was invented by people who had no proper weapons. It developed in time as a way to protect an unarmed man from a man with a weapon. Then you use your bare hands, trained and strengthened, to subdue him. Often you can best him just by helping him to go in the direction he has chosen, using to your advantage his body weight, his momentum. Or you strike him a disabling blow. It's a practical science, jiujitsu. It's not a theoretical exercise. Not a game like boxing, with a rule that allows you to strike only with your closed hands. It's not a sport. It's fighting in dead earnest. Here. Come away from that bench. I'll show you something useful."

I did not much like the lecture, but I was always interested in the sort of thing he seemed to be talking about—interested in a wholly theoretical way, I'm afraid. I stood up and went towards him.

"Now, I want you to throw a left at me. Take it easy, we're not here to batter each other. Let's see your left, easy now."

I turned quartering to him, put up my hands, and in slow motion, dead slow, I mimicked a straight left. I started to turn my hand over, straightened my arm, began to tighten my hand into a fist, and I was just locking the elbow with my hand four inches from his face — I meant to go no farther — when his right arm struck my forearm up and away, hard.

What . . .

He took a step forward. He was about an inch taller than I, and much heavier. Now I saw his eyes some three inches higher than mine. I thought, He's up on his toes. What . . . I don't remember seeing him strike. But I know what he did. The right arm that had knocked away my sham punch rose higher still as he came forward, and then he struck me with the edge of his rigid hand on the muscle between my neck and the point of my shoulder. The sensation was like the concussion of a hand grenade or a mortar round or a shell exploding close by. The sunlight was extinguished, I could not see. There was no feeling on my right side all the way down to my foot and I thought that I had fainted standing. After a time, I heard him talking, but I could not catch what he said. Then, slowly, the light began to seep back. I could not stir for my paralyzed right side, but now I could understand the words. "I'm really surprised. When I deliver a chop like that I expect to see the man fall. I'm really surprised." I knew why I had not fallen. In executing my part of the demonstration I had slipped my left foot forward as my hand went towards him. It was still on the same spot. Had I had my feet together I should certainly have fallen. As it was, with my sight coming back and my head registering what his talk meant, I found that I was swaying. "Never seen a case like that. Very surprised." The numbness was beginning to be an uncertain ache. I told myself, wonderingly, that he had meant to fell me like a tree, just as if he had not said as much. I told myself that I must get to that bench, but not limping. He had meant to fell me, he a grown man, something over two hundred pounds. It was beyond belief. Now I thought that I could walk, and I walked most deliberately to the table, rounded the table, and with great care stepped over the bench, left leg first, then right leg, and sat down. My right shoulder and my arm seemed still to be no part of my body, but they were giving me signs, from a distance, tingling and pricking. He had meant to fell me. With every repetition I marveled less. I felt somehow removed from myself, and now that my heart had stopped its horrid thumping, almost calm. He went on talking.

"Now, where would you be in a real fight, even though you were still on your feet after taking that chop? You could be dead three times over before you recovered yourself. Boxing—it isn't worth a cuntful of chipped ice if you have to stand against a man trained in jiujitsu." He was folding his wet clothes over the line without fastening them in any way; there was no wind. He had filled quite a bit of the clothesline with his washing, and the rest of the line was out of easy reach. I had picked up my pen as soon as my hand had got some feeling in it, just to keep myself in countenance. I was looking down at the paper with only the date upon it. But I could hear him coming towards me. To my astonishment I heard him mount the bench to my left. He was still talking. I had to admire his style; he seemed not to bear me a grudge at all for the blow that he had dealt me. He was really quite cordial, though earnest about his jiu-jitsu doctrine. "Boxing," he said. "It's not worth a cuntful of cold water." He pronounced the letter *t* with a clarity that eludes the slack and genial Americans. Mostly I find it detestable when foreigners say in my language the forbidden words in common use, because their odd accent—odd to me—makes those words obscene. But this time I was only dimly annoyed. Could I hold his heel on the bench with my numb right hand? That was the question. I opened and closed it gently. Perhaps I could.

I looked up at him for the first time to see what he was doing with the hitch on the trunk of the palm tree, and how far along he was with it. He was hauling on the line to gain some slack so that he could slide the hitch where he wanted it. Now he drew back his hands from their work. I bent towards him, grasped his heel with my right hand, found his kneecap with my left, and shoved that knee with all the strength I had.

The result was beyond what I had hoped. I had seen that takedown performed, I had done it myself, but only when the subject was standing on the ground. My Australian had been perched on a bench some eighteen inches high. He cleared the table completely, flying backward, and pitched heavily onto one shoulder. He was at such a distance that I could see all of him, from his head to his feet, beyond the table, beyond the bench on its farther side. He lay on his back, not stirring.

I felt no emotion, not even satisfaction. It did not occur to me that if the throw had not worked he could have throttled me. I was not yet sufficiently recovered. I looked down at the page, picked up the pen, and wrote, "Dear Dad."

Nothing came to me after that. I have no idea how much time had gone by before he spoke. He said, "Yank, you play rough." I didn't look up.

After some moments he said, "I can't move."

That seemed to rouse me. I said slowly, "When I manhandle someone in that way he generally breaks his neck. What you have is no more than a broken shoulder. I'm surprised."

He said, "Here, I can't move. Help me up."

I got up very slowly. My limbs seemed to be working. I stepped free of the bench. I walked over to him, and I sank down and squatted. That went well. Then I put my forefinger on the place where the bridge of his nose joined his forehead. He closed his eyes when he saw the finger approach. When I touched him he opened them again.

"In the state you're in I could kill you in several interesting ways. For example, if I were to strike you with the edge of my hand on this spot, using only a tenth of the force with which you struck me, you would die in three or four hours, and during all that while you would not be able to speak." I had heard that somewhere. It might have been true. "I know half a dozen ways to kill you that would give you plenty of time to think." That was a fabrication. "If I help you, you're a dead man." That one I meant.

I stood up and went back to my bench.

Some time later, two Australians came up.

"What's happened to him. Is he crook?"

"He hurt himself."

"Why didn't you help him up?"

"He doesn't want me to help him."

They looked at each other. One said, "Jack, you stay here. I'll get two other jokers and we'll take him away." And he went off.

The man called Jack looked at the man on the ground. He looked at me, and he looked away as if he had seen something ugly. In a little while his mate was back, and there were two men with him. The two looked at me and looked away. As they bent down to him, the man who had gone for recruits said, "Where are you hurt, mate? We want to lift you easy." The man on the ground said, "I don't know. I don't feel anything. He says I have a broken shoulder." The two men at his head felt under him, but he gave no sign, and they grasped him under the armpits. The other two took up his lower legs, and together they carried him away.

I NEVER saw him again. He must have been taken to some base hospital, American or Australian. No one troubled me about his accident. I imagine that a man trained in jiujitsu would not inform the doctor that a boy had broken his shoulder for him. Now, he was a species of madman, the prophet of a cause, as serenely oblivious as a scientist. He had no notion that he had broken the bond of trust that holds the world together. Science must prevail, and in his person. Clearly, he had played that trick before, and no one had thought to kill him for it. It seems to me that Pudd'nhead Wilson's axiom applies here: "He ought to be underground, inspiring the cabbages." At the time, what he had done made a great impression upon me. I thought his breach of faith something unnameable. And yet that looks rather different to me now. Since that time I have seen it often. I had thought him a human sport, in the breeder's term, but his trouble was not necessarily genetic. You can learn to behave like that. At this moment we are entering into a disgraceful war, the criminals on both sides having been rendered impervious to the horror that must ensue. The principals in this projected slaughter have no excuse. (I speak now of my scoundrel countrymen. I cannot take responsibility for foreign malefactors.) I speak of our American statesmen because they have all had university educations. The American scoundrels, then, put into perspective for me the man who a year later, sitting beside me in a bar in newly liberated Manila, a man to whom I had not spoken, stabbed me with a narrow-bladed dagger. I had turned my head to the right to look at something or other when I felt the stir beside me on my left. I moved my shoulder into whatever he was doing, and that made the downward stab, aimed to go behind the collarbone—a fine place to cut arteries—strike instead the upper arm where it joins the shoulder. He was surprised, and he pulled his hand away from the haft. I plucked out the knife and gave it back to him promptly, and then I left that place because I did not want to find out what the military government might make of it. Now, that man was poor. He was underfed. He had not had the benefit of a university. He had lived through the terror of the Japanese occupation. He was mad, or perhaps a professional thief who stole with violence, a sorry trade. To what the world's chancellors are preparing now, what passed between that man and me was the merest mopery: spitting on the high seas, stabbing a horse and stealing his blanket. But it is a dismal thing when the people's elected representatives, elected to perform certain clerkly tasks for us, take to ruling the citizens. That is the breach of faith that has gone on for generations, especially pernicious in our country because the open character of public administration, the habit of saying aloud whatever you please, makes the Americans loth to charge the government with usurpation. The last time the nation woke up was when it discovered that it had been bombing Cambodia—which all the world knew, except for the trusting American press—fourteen years into the war in Vietnam. And shortly after that, Watergate. At which point the rulers of the people had to profess themselves shocked, and to make a show of impeaching the arch-ruler.

But back to murder, on a homely, artisanal scale. César Vallejo is a most eloquent poet. I have a friend, ditto, who translated nobly a poem of Vallejo. My friend's version is copyrighted, so I must give you, condensed, the prose of it. The poet says, "Sometimes there comes to me a feeling of boundless plenitude, and I want then to make sympathy active, and understanding active. Even helping the killer to kill—terrible thought. And what this desire comes down to is to be always straight with my conscience."

In fine, the heroism of the modern poet. Auden puts the best face on it: "Follow poet, follow right / to the bottom of the night." But Vallejo's extreme posture is an awkward one. Five will get you ten if Vallejo ever helped the killer kill anyone. I know that my friend's hands have no blood upon them. I think Vallejo is slumming, spiritually speaking. He wants in good conscience to register with his conscience the thrill he is experiencing in the imaginary lower depths. Like the fat boy in *Pickwick* he wants to make your flesh creep. And very likely his own.

Long before my friend knew of Vallejo, as I take it, he wrote (and damn copyright):

The killer has a belly and balls, like mine.
The soles of his feet sweat, like mine.
I'm in a hardening world, like his.
The world's full of my kills. I've every
weaker man in my helpless grasp, like him.

How much manlier, the confession of helpless complicity. It defines, and goes some way to redeem, fallen man.

It does not imply a generous, warm-hearted collaboration with the killer, poor fellow. Vallejo's *mot* lends itself to universalization; you could build a cartel with it: help the pimp to pimp, the slavemaster to enslave—terrible thought. At the top of the pyramid the Nestlé company. There's millions in it.

The trouble with murder, practical and theoretical, is that you grow callous. That sounds anticlimactic, not to say comical. But there are millions of persons in the world whose business it is to kill: soldiers, police, judges who pronounce the death sentence, persons who carry out the sentence, and on and on. Their practices make all the world callous, so that killing is a custom. Only a few benighted tribes of primitives lack the custom. For the rest of us, we may not every day have the opportunity to snuff out a life, but there are plenty of occasions for brutality that goes some way in that direction. The Army called me up during the war in Korea, and I was in a training regiment. One day my platoon was waiting, after a classroom discussion, to do some practice killing with mortars. I like weapons of all sorts, but I loathed mortars at first sight. There appeared to be some mix-up in the expanses of Jersey sand; someone said that men from quite another regiment had the mortars, and we would have to wait our turn. Our lieutenant was a man who liked to see things for himself. He ordered me to take charge of bayonet drill for the platoon while he reconnoitered the alien regiment. There were no ragged stuffed dummies to stab, and at first I was at a loss to carry out the drill, but I had said, "Yes, Sir," as he strode to the encounter. This was in the afternoon of a hot July day. I formed the men into a single rank abreast, and had them go through the business of advancing, retreating, parrying, delivering the quietus with the bayonet point, and the grace note with the butt of the rifle to the enemy's head. To inspirit them, I did the drill myself, standing at right angles to them, at a prudent distance. It was heavy work in the heat. The rifle weighed ten pounds, the bayonet nearly two, and you had to foin before you with that heavy instrument, sometimes at arm's length. I was the oldest man in the platoon, used to physical exertion. The seventeen-year-olds who made up the largest number felt it like the wrath of God. After fifteen minutes I was convinced and the platoon was exhausted. I told the men to stand at ease.

So we all grounded arms, red-faced, sweating, exclaiming, complaining. Then the lieutenant arrived. I suppose that he had had no success with the officer in possession.

He was certainly in a temper. He demanded to know why we were not at bayonet drill, an exercise that someday might save our worthless lives. I said that we had gone through the drill and that I was giving the platoon a breather; he could see that we were all in a sweat. That made him angrier. The worst of it was that I had told the men to unfix bayonets and sheathe them. He told me that it was irresponsible not to keep the men drilling when it was a matter of life and death. He had expected a little more sense of duty on my part and a little more sense, period. He and I were at a little remove from the platoon, and that led me into trouble. I thought I could make the lieutenant see reason; he was very decent, though an officer. In a low voice I told him he must know that the bayonet was virtually useless, because only a severely injured man would let you bayonet him. I was a fencer, and if, equipped with rifle and bayonet, I found an enemy in the same case, I would have some idea of how to cope with him. But if he approached me barehanded I would flee for my life; the leverage would be all against me. I said this with many Sirs. But when I came to the end of my speech he bounded over to the platoon. "Give me your rifle," he said to the man nearest him. Then, "Your bayonet." He fixed it in place as smooth as silk—he was admirably coordinated—and he told me to hand over my rifle to that man.

"Now," he said, "how's that again? You'd drop the rifle and run if a man approached you barehanded?"

"Not drop the rifle," I began. But he was already executing a swift, elegant lunge at my chest. I was only just in time to slap the bayonet aside. In the same motion I seized the muzzle of the rifle with my left hand, put my right hand just forward of the trigger guard, and took the weapon away from him. Then, somewhat carried away, I struck him with the butt on his helmet liner, not really hard. The blow knocked him off his feet, but he was up in an instant and coming towards me. I offered the rifle to him nearly at present arms, the bayonet pointed at the sky. "Sir, I'm the one who's in danger now. You can take this away from me just as easily as I took it from you." He stopped short. "Private, you know this is court-martial stuff." I said, "Sir, if I had been just a little slower I would have a hole in my chest right now." He thought for a moment. "All right. Let's forget it."

That was very decent for an officer whose authority had been questioned by an underling, and before all those men. He was certainly unusual. And there were two other things for me to think about. First, no one in my platoon ever remarked on that bit of byplay. I decided that the boys must have had no interest at all in that brief discussion of tactics; it was as if, in their minds, they were not about to go to war. The other question was why had I added that last fillip, the butt-stroke to the head. It was, of course, part of the ritual of bayonet drill, just like yelling. But I remembered very clearly that after I had secured that rifle I thought, I've gone this far, now I'll follow through. And after the slightest hesitation I tapped his helmet liner with peculiar satisfaction. I had wanted to see him fall to the ground.

These impulses become a habit. They seem quite natural, and when you act on them they bring a kind of pleasure, like the pleasure of good workmanship. As if a man were not as fragile as an egg.

I SAW Morgan and his friend a number of times, but I was sure that I was in no danger from them. To a man, the population of the camp avoided me, especially the Australians, who no longer greeted me with their automatic "Goodday." It was as if I had got something awful, something catching. That would have been intolerable if it had lasted, but I was given a mission by the port authorities, that is, the U.S. Army. I was to take charge of a convoy of ten landing barges and bring them safely to Finschhafen, some five days' journey up the coast, as they reckoned. The barges each had a very large ramp that was the bow, and it could be lowered onto a gently sloping beach to give footing to disembarking troops. That ramp was an eyesore to a seaman. It made a lot of sail area in the wrong place, and it also offered poor visibility dead ahead. Each barge had twin diesel engines and no accommodation for the contemplated cruise.

I assumed that the military authorities had not heard that I was in Coventry for vicious conduct. I assumed that their choice had fallen on me because of my personal virtue. So I told the officers of the port that every barge ought to have a wooden framework on which could be spread a canvas shelter deck to keep the crew out of the wet during their watch below. They had already thought of having in each barge a man who could steer and navigate, and two men who could see to the care and feeding of the diesels. They were a little surprised at my suggesting that Jack would want to sleep dry, but they took it well. They promised to provide the carpentry and the canvas. In the event, the crews of each barge had to do the carpentry, but it's the thought that counts. I asked for Danforth anchors (not designed for coral bottoms, as it turned out), manila anchor lines, rations, and charts. I asked for guns, since no one seemed to know where the remaining Japanese units might be. They agreed to everything but firearms, saying that it was counter to regulations. I think they expected that we would shoot ourselves in the foot.

While they were outfitting the barges for the voyage, and when the framing for the shelter deck was in place on each vessel, I had nothing to do but study the charts. These dated from the seventies and eighties of the last century and had been prepared by survey vessels of the British navy. The frequent notation, "Position doubtful," referring to reefs, rocks, and small islands, did not inspire confidence. Even more troubling was the not uncommon "Existence doubtful." My orders were to show no lights if we happened to sail at night, and it made me wonder. If we were to creep along the coast of New Guinea, on soundings, indeed almost within hailing distance of the shore—and we must do something like that because the barges were by no means good sea-boats—then the problem of keeping stations, or even keeping count of the vessels, was severe. They must have been thinking of convoys of large vessels in the open sea, if they were thinking of anything. And if we were not to betray our presence at night, what were we to do in daylight? I raised the point and the officers told me that the orders came from higher authority. Then I spoke of what had been working at me from the first, without my having been aware of it. What man would relieve the helmsman who must also be doing the piloting, inshore navigation? Though I could set a course, and the convoy would follow more or less in my wake, anything like heavy weather would be bound to scatter the vessels and put each very much on its own. Aboard these barges the helmsman was the skipper, and it was imprudent to give him no relief, for the men who took the engine watches by turns were not seamen in the same sense. Losing contact at night could be disastrous. The officers said that the orders came from upstairs, and they could not question them.

At this point we were two days from shoving off. I was thinking that I would make sure to get to Finschhafen by very easy stages. The bridge on those barges was a steel box open to the sky, its walls reaching about chest height. The controls were the ignition switch and two throttles. The vessel was steered by giving more power to one screw or less to the other. That was an efficient system, even when backing, but it was unpleasant because the throttle handles were very stiff, so that you could not slow or accelerate smoothly. And the roar of the engines reverberated mercilessly in the steel hull. Eight hours conning the barge would be very hard work in unfamiliar waters, and hardest for mother's little lambkin, who had the overall responsibility for the flotilla.

I was thinking these things while wandering in the bamboo grove. It was full of crisscross paths that were really game trails; the tracks of wild pigs were everywhere. I had come about a half-mile among the bamboo stems, steering a relatively straight course by the sun. All at once I heard clicking sounds to my front, seemingly quite close by. I was not much posted on the habits of the pig, and I remembered seeing wicked tusks worn as a necklace by one of the rightful owners of that soil. I retreated immediately and followed my back trail, trying to be as quiet as possible. After ten minutes of that I began to feel more comfortable, and I turned my thoughts again to that convoy. I was pleased to have been given my first command, and as commodore at that. While I was congratulating myself in that way, stepping along briskly, suddenly I saw part of a clearing before me and slightly to one side. It had been obscured by three very slender bamboo trunks. Two men were in that clearing, one leaning against a palm, one squatting down beside him. The standing figure was partly in profile. *Caput apri*—I stopped dead. I felt a nasty pang as my heart took alarm. Slowly I moved aside to put a slim bamboo between the clearing and me, and moved again to take shelter behind two more bamboo, till I could back away into the thicket out of sight. I knew that the cordovan man and his friend were under a great misapprehension, certain that I was crazy and dangerous. But I could not put away panic until by a circuit I had made my way out of the grove. And I had no clue to what had troubled me. I think now that I had guessed that man's trouble, without any understanding of what it was that I knew. He kept up a bold front always, with much expense of energy. The painful effort had come to feel comfortable and comforting to him, and the cramp of domination relieved his fear. In the way that a dedicated cynic cheapens life, dousing the light for all around him, that man generated self-distrust. Naturally timid and uncertain, I was fearful of contamination. Only enmity could keep up my courage in his presence. And now that he was in a sense defeated I was mortally afraid.

TWO DAYS later we took our departure from the sole seamark, an old oil drum a few hundred feet from shore, tethered to the bottom for some purpose patently not related to navigation. Our huge bow-ramps breasted an easy tide making from the mouth of the bay. It was raining, but the visibility was better than one mile, and turning about in the iron box I counted my ducklings swimming valiantly, dipping and rising to the small seas inspired by the onshore breeze. All in all the little ships had an air that I found quite *coquet.*

As we cleared the bay and struck the long sea swell, the barges rolled, but not so much as to expose the screws. I wondered what speed we might be making over the ground as we turned to follow the coastline, drawing abeam of the north headland. I could not do anything in the way of chart work; both hands were needed on the throttle levers most of the time if I was to steer a reasonable course. At arm's length my fingers span fifteen degrees, and I was about to do rough geometry on the headland with that instrument when it struck me that any gesture of the kind would be seen at least by the helmsman of the first barge astern. He would be puzzled, wondering what I was pointing at, and with what intention. We had signal flags, but again I was not free to wigwag at him in Morse or semaphore. I cursed the complacency of the people who had done us out of the shipmates who could take the helm by turns with us and in a transe like this help with the piloting problems and send signals through the long flotilla sailing in line ahead. And then the sun broke through the clouds, pouring down a column of light. The sea changed from bronze to blue. Even at half-throttle the diesels roared and whined, but all was elation in the lead barge.

Some three hours later I decided that we had had our shakedown cruise. I began to examine the main and the offshore islands with a purpose. I needed to study the charts and see how they tallied with the landmarks, since seamarks there were none. The place I found for landing was a bight on an island whose shore was protected by coral reefs. There was a cable-length of placid water at one place, and I steered for it. No one had told us that the coral did not rise where the fresh water met the salt, but I grew familiar with that wonder during the cruise. As we passed in line through the broad gap in the coral, we could see the breakers on either hand, then we noticed the course of the freshwater stream on the foreshore, then the coco palms, and at last the houses built on pilings at the tidemark. I steered to port for the beach, waving to the barge astern to follow on the starboard hand. The clever helmsman made the same gesture to the next barge, and in a short time ten ramps lay on the coral sands.

Since we were trespassers in that part of the world, I thought we should make an official visit to the village and give an account of ourselves. One man in the lead barge was indisposed, a little seasick from diesel fumes and the unaccustomed motion of a quite small vessel in a seaway. The other fellow was sound. He and I took turns carrying half a gunnysack of tinned bully beef; we had a generous supply, and we had been informed that the stuff was an eligible present. Indeed the people received us kindly. They wanted to give us two mangoes for every can of beef. When we protested, as envoys must, they pointed out that we were thirty, one man taking my hand gently and making the tally on my fingers.

They were canoe men, with powerful chests and arms, and quite slim legs, except for the one man who had elephantiasis, his foot and the lower part of his left leg monstrously swollen, which didn't hurt the working of him. He walked up a coco palm, bent double, the afflicted foot and the good one against the trunk and his hands on the far side of it, merely out of courtesy, in order to throw down to us some coconuts for drinking. The women wore ample grass skirts, but we affected not to see them at all because all their upper bodies were bare. So we returned to the flotilla richer than before, both in goods and in sentiment. We had been chucker with bully beef, our constant ration. We were vaguely troubled because we could remark the musculature of the men, sculpted by the paddle, but we must turn our eyes from the breasts of the women.

We called a muster, firstly to whack out the mangoes and then to consult. The charts showed a long stretch before the next reasonable anchorage, and in order to get there we must thread our way through cumbered waters. It appeared to me that the difficulty of judging our speed—we had no patent log, not even a chip log—and the unknown set and speed of the coastal currents could have us aground. We could not take accurate bearings but must steer at a venture, watching mostly the color of the water and the wave shapes. These were an argument for sailing before sundown and through the night because the chart showed deep water and a coast largely mountainous and steep-to before we would come to the troublesome patches that we really must traverse in full daylight. A number of the pilots had already come to that conclusion. The weather promised to be clear, and though it was the dark of the moon the starlight would be a good help. We agreed to set out while the sun was strong so as to steer safely through the breach in the coral.

AT TWO in the morning the sea and the barge came alight. I looked up and saw a descending flare lighting from below the underside of the aircraft that had dropped it. For a moment I made myself small in my iron box. I told myself in Irish, They're after killing me, and me not nineteen. I expected machine-gun fire on our barge, the more so because I could not hear the airplane's engine for the roaring of our own. After a few seconds and nothing happening, I looked up again. It was one of those light aircraft that were used for artillery spotting—or for chivvying a convoy of barges—looking like a Piper or a Taylor. The flare fell into the sea close aboard. Then I remembered that there was almost no chance of a Japanese aircraft operating on that stretch of the coast. It must be one of ours. The pilot had dropped his flare right near the lead barge. He must have seen by starlight the white wakes of the vessels. But what had he hoped to discover with that flare, a display of Japanese ensigns? I was the more incensed because I had numbly given myself up for lost, with the half-formed thought that the canvas deck could give no protection to the poor fellows below. What price running without lights now? But after a few minutes of scornful reflections the incident trickled away. Dropping that flare was foolish, but a man a mile high in the air must find it hard to take seriously a line of water beetles on the surface of the sea. I began to wonder what the men in the other barges thought of the business. Had they been alarmed? And then, for the first time, it came to me that my mates had not been shunning me since we had landed on the island now astern. I was pleased that it was so, but incurious — I scarcely ever see the issue when it arises. I think now that everyone understood that we were making a passage under conditions that the authorities at Milne Bay did not understand at all, and we must all pull together. And without noticing, I had been forced to relinquish my standing as a virtuous outcast.

For five days, we threaded our way through many reefs, and once through a flume made by the steep mountains of the coast and a small mountain that was a half-drowned volcano with many reefs to seaward. Those reefs were so extensive that we chose to try the flume. The wind blew fiercely between the island and the main, against what must have been a five-knot current. But then we found ourselves in safe waters again. We thought to make Finschhafen by six o'clock in the evening, with good daylight still. This was child's play. However, after three hours it came on to blow, and we were skirting a lee shore that was alternately sheer rock or low-lying ground defended by coral. I began to steer quartering into the wind so as to gain searoom. Everything seemed straightforward still, though the seas were turning into combers. Looking astern to see if the flotilla was following in our wake, I was surprised to find that two of the vessels were more than a mile behind the body of the convoy. I turned about at once, taking a dollop of sea that poured off the canvas shelter into our living quarters; the black gang popped up immediately to see if we were foundering. As we passed each barge, I slowed and then stopped the engines, signing to the helmsman to do the same. Then I shouted to him to steer slow ahead into the wind, pointing then to the two vessels that had fallen behind. When we drew up to those boats they were steering to follow the course from which we had departed only a little while ago, but they were making scant headway. Then I saw that the last barge of the convoy was low in the water, and one of the crew was bailing with a bucket. The other vessel was standing by. The puzzle was where the water could be coming from, given the vessel's steel plates and new seacocks.

The vessel keeping company with the stricken one steered to within a hundred feet of us. The helmsman cut his engines and we did too. He shouted that on that barge the engines' cooling water was being somehow diverted inboard. The cooling-water hose had already been under water when the crew had taken notice. The hose was in an awkward place and it was hard to find the damage, feeling with one's hands in semidarkness. Then we began to drift apart. I told him to start his engines slow and to keep company with us while the rest of the convoy was marking time.

We approached the vessel, logy with its load of seawater. I shouted to the helmsman to stop engines, since they seemed to be pumping water into the ship. I told him to stand by to take a heaving line, make it fast to his anchor cable, and let out a hundred feet of scope between us to make a tow line. He said he preferred a wire rope, and he would send the eye of it to me with the heaving line. I didn't like the idea; wire has no give to it, and when his vessel was toiling to rise to a sea and our boat sliding down another, there could be ructions. I shouted that the sea was rough and would put sudden strains on the wire. He grew angry and yelled something that I could not make out. But as we drew closer, I heard, "Who died and left you boss of the Pacific? I'm in command of this hooker. Morgan had your number. I'm not afraid of you, you maniac." I could feel the grateful flood of hatred rising in me. All right, you bastard. I coiled the heaving line and threw it. The wind was from me to him, and the line sailed right over his iron box. To my regret the monkey-fist with three steel nuts in it for ballast did not even graze his head as it went by.

By the time he had clapped his wire on a pair of his forward bitts and made fast the heaving line to the other eye, the wind had turned us so that one of the pair of bitts on our stern was handy to secure it. I slipped it over the bitts at once because with our lighter draft we were bearing down upon him and we must pull away. I started the engines, slow, to take up the slack. His barge began to move with ours, though at an angle, and I opened the throttles a bit.

Some two minutes later I heard a sound like a kettledrum. I spun around and saw that wire coming towards us, and that fellow's bitts were not on the barge but catapulting in the air. I had thought the wire might become stranded and dangerous when we had a sea between the two boats. I had not imagined that the bitts had simply been tack-welded to the steel deck. So much for wartime shipbuilding. In the rising wind it took five minutes to maneuver so as to put the heaving line athwart the other barge again, and the line drifted far forward with the wind until it hung up on the vessel's ramp. The helmsman had to clamber forward on the narrow steel deck, with nothing useful to hold on to. When he captured the line he turned and yelled, "And you call yourself a seaman." Most dexterously—I think because he was in a rage—he made his way aft on the pitching deck, hauled in his wire, and dropped the eye on the other pair of bitts on his stern. That fitting tore out too after a few hard jerks. We tried it a third time on a pair of his forward bitts with the same result. I shouted to the man that he had one more pair of bitts, and I would send my manila anchor cable to him with the heaving line. He did not answer. I came nearly alongside to leeward of him. He hauled in the cable, made a bowline in it, and flung the loop onto the bitts. I slacked out a long scope, secured the cable at my end, and started slow ahead.

When I looked around me I found that we had drifted near the shore. There was heavy surf along a hollow in the shoreline, and steering somewhat to windward to correct our leeway, I hoped to pass parallel to the reefs and find an opening. The towed barge came along quietly enough on its three-inch manila tether, and it did not seem to me to be settling further. But for all I knew it might sink at any moment. It would be very hard to pick up its crew with the sea in that state. And if it did sink suddenly it might be impossible to cast off the anchor line swiftly enough on our own barge, with the weight of the sinking vessel on the bitts.

We seemed to be moving very slowly. I wondered if there was an adverse current holding us back as well as the dead weight of the disabled boat. There was a large wrench at my feet that I had forgotten to stow, and I bent down to pick it up. I struck the steel bulkhead three times with the wrench, and the sound brought two heads out from under the canvas. I signed to them to come to me. One started towards me immediately. The other, my fellow ambassador to the islanders, nodded but turned back for a moment. A particularly heavy sea made the boat roll and pitch at the same time, and another came, and another. At that point my two mates were bent over, clinging to the coaming of the hold. Then there was a smooth, and they came up swiftly. Even at close range I had to shout over the noise of the engines. When they looked astern they understood at once. I asked that one of them stand beside me, looking aft to give me notice if the other vessel seemed to be sinking. The other man I told to go forward, climb the ramp, and signal to me if he saw an opening in the coral. That ramp would be a dangerous perch, and he knew it, but he started forward. Then I had to shout to him to come back, for I had just made out the opening myself. In a quarter of an hour we were in calm water with a bright coral bottom. The wind was blowing directly into the harbor, but with much less force. Twenty minutes later we had maneuvered the towed barge to where it could drop its ramp upon the sand, and all the other vessels were at anchor.

In a short time we had six men in the boat, all bailing, and we were sweating to some purpose for the water dropped noticeably. I was cheek by jowl with the commander, both of us too busy for recriminations or even for thoughts. In half an hour we found that the cooling-water hose was intact; the pump was at fault. That was, of course, the diagnosis of the engineers, Greek to me. Then they announced that it was easy to set it right again. And that was the end of the adventure.

Except that, after nightfall, we saw something remarkable. A canoe approached us quietly. The man in the bow held a smouldering torch. He swung it in a circle now and again, and each time he did that it burst into flame. When the canoe came closer we saw that he held the torch in his left hand and a spear was in his right. In the stern was a small boy. He was the motive power; I guessed he might be six years old. He paddled noiselessly, with a kind of sculling, never lifting his paddle from the water. The canoe had an outrigger on the starboard side. Its weight kept the little boat from rolling the portside under, and its buoyancy kept the starboard gunwale from shipping water. The canoe was exceedingly slender. Its greatest beam was at the waterline. From the waterline to the gunwale it had a great deal of tumblehome — the boy in the stern and the man in the bow each sat upon both gunwales at once, and these were so close together that they kept one knee before the other. It was as if a fourteen-foot cigar had a long slit in its top surface. At one moment, when they were within thirty feet of us, the man said something in a tone that sounded harsh, as if the boy had made a serious error. At any rate we saw the child start. Immediately afterwards, he did something in that odd, noiseless sculling fashion of his, and it moved the boat broadside to port for at least five or six feet. It was astonishing to us. Physics does not work that way for American canoeists. Then the man stood upright in an easy fluid motion, swung his torch, stabbed the water with his spear, and pulled up from the dark lagoon a fish three feet long. He thrust the quivering fish into the canoe behind him. Then he quenched his torch in the water, and the boy moved the little vessel away into the night.

We sailed before dawn for Finschhafen. After a run of some five hours we rounded a small cape and found the broad harbor. There were many ships at anchor in the basin, the most imposing a heavy cruiser flying the Australian ensign. The crew had been mustered for Sunday services, and with the band they sang a hymn that was made musical and touching by the distance. As we brought up to an anchor the band began to play the quickstep, and we saw the sailors marching and countermarching among the guns. Just yesterday we had gained with much difficulty a remote and placid harbor. This morning we were slipping easily and naturally into the bosom of the war.

STARING AT THE SUN

I AM NOT given to shedding tears, even when the circumstances might seem to authorize them. Of course I don't count the movies. In the dark theater, images larger than life flashing before you, a solemn music working on the nerves, and the actor's misery calling up the pain of every life, tears will come.

Some time ago there was a perfect rash of my young relatives getting married. Who weeps at weddings? In my experience, the mother of the bride, the mother of the groom, and I. Following attentively the rites I do not honor on working days, I hear the poetry of hope. And I break down, just as in the movies. No matter how badly the officiant reads from Scripture.

But on the whole I do not weep. I have heard of persons who wept for joy, but I do not remember seeing an instance of that. I have seen people weep for enthusiasm. An example: my shipmate Tony Zak and I blew into Galveston—

literally, there was a gale blowing on that coast—and we declined into the YMCA. Tony was a coal miner when we did not have a world war. He had lost the tips of three fingers of his left hand in the Pennsylvania mines, but he liked the trade. He said that no one ever bothered you underground. What with all the explosives lying around, people were inclined to be polite down in the pit. Tony represented the third generation of Polish miners in the States, and as it happened we had set down our seabags on two bunks that were near to that of a young man who was a Polish Pole, and a seaman, too. He had called out a greeting, and Tony had heard beneath his pleasant English what his native tongue must be. The foreign sailor came over to us smiling, a well-knit, spirited fellow with fine dark eyes. I watched the two for a moment as they chatted in Polish, and then I turned to stowing my gear. I looked up suddenly as Tony seemed to reel away from the other man. "What's the matter?" Tears were streaming down his face. The words came out strangled. "He speaks such beautiful Polish."

Years later I heard from a classmate a story that went the other way. It seemed to me to be the pendant to Tony's emotion, which was complicated, no doubt, as if he had felt how splendid, how painful, to hear the mother tongue uncorrupted by three generations of Pennsylvania. My classmate's given name was Hugh, and he was called Hughie, even by himself. That was astonishing because he was unbending in almost every other matter. I was in a colloquium with him once, and it struck me that whatever topic was touched on he knew more about it than the two amiable professors, and he drew conclusions that seemed more sound and more original. He was of a saturnine temper. He posed as a cynic. I thought it meant that he expected good things to befall him always but was sometimes disappointed by the Fates — an acute form of the sentimentality of self. But that might have been too clever a diagnosis. I remember mentioning to him the costs of the Russian Revolution, the mass deportations, the mass killings. He said, "Your opinion is childish. Have you thought about the problem that any revolutionary group would have to face if it inherited the remains of imperial Russia? How do you wring from an impoverished peasantry — nine-tenths of the population — a surplus that will allow you to invest in modernization, in industrialization? You have to starve that peasantry further, mulcting it of a portion of its already inadequate ration. And when they are recalcitrant you have to shoot them. I'd like to see you govern and modernize a country like that, with your fatuous views." I thought, Why bother with a revolution if that's what's required? But Hughie did state the problem of the revolutionaries on their own terms. He did not pretend that things were going along just dandy in the Soviet Union, which was all that I had ever heard from people who were sympathetic to the regime. Except for Wilmer Stone, my teacher in high school, who said, "That is government by murder. If I were in their place I couldn't bear it. I just hope they get beyond the heroic phase very soon and develop benign civil government." But he was a most unusual man.

Hughie's major was in history. He had taught himself half the languages of Europe so that he could find out at first hand what this or that nation thought it was up to—as a corrective to what we thought of it, or failed to think. At one time he signed up for a seminar in contemporary French literature. When I showed surprise he said, "Novels give you better history and better sociology." He turned in a term paper on Malraux, in French, since the seminar was conducted in that language. Then he received a note asking him to meet with the professors who led the seminar. Hughie told me that they were polite but they knew for certain that he had had assistance in writing his paper. One said that the essay had been proofread very carefully—there was not a single accent mark misplaced or incorrect. The other said that, beyond the immaculate orthography, his French wife was sure that the paper had been written by a mature scholar who was French, and not by an American undergraduate. Hughie said, "I can do that in at least five languages, *pace* your lady wife, and I thank her for her flattering opinion." He proposed that they set him another topic, giving him an hour to deal with it. They assented at once, Hughie told me, because they thought the trial would damn him at once. They came back in an hour and a half—

how's that for fair? Or perhaps it had more to do with the indolent custom of the *akademische Viertelstunde*, and they just couldn't make that formation on time. They found Hughie with his feet up on the desk and a five-page essay completed—*sans rature*. "I rose courteously," Hughie said. The professors read the first page, leafed through the rest, apologized, congratulated him. Hughie told me, "They must not have heard anything I said all semester. And I took that seminar for a ridiculous reason. One of those guys loved Montaigne enough to translate him *in extenso*, three volumes' worth." The incident got him something he had coveted, a closed fellowship established by our university at one of the Oxford colleges. He might not have been noticed otherwise.

I asked Hughie how he had felt at the moment of vindication. "I didn't feel a thing. I said good-bye to those gentlemen. But as I was walking in the quad I burst out laughing. I laughed aloud. People stared at me. I couldn't stop. I was whooping."

I said sympathetically, "You were that elated."

"Elated? Elated my foot. That was scorn and rage. I laughed hysterically at the way the world wags."

Four months after the operation—pardon me, four months after the Procedure—perhaps because of the January thaw that allowed her to feel somewhat less uncertain on her feet, Diana said that we really ought to visit my parents in Spain. "They're getting on. The family is long-lived, but your mother and father are getting on. You want to have the good of them while they're still around." We flew to Málaga, ten or a dozen miles from the hill town where my people were sojourning in luxury of a kind because Spain is the country of the poor. Well, they were not throwing money about in the casinos of the Costa del Sol, they lived very modestly, but the sea, the sun, the presence of mannerly Spaniards were tonic to them. It was a good place for an old gent and an old lady to be, as opposed, say, to the city of New York. Some two years earlier my father was on a subway platform in that city, just settling himself on a bench to wait for the train. Three teenaged girls came up, and each gave him a smart blow on the head with her umbrella as she passed. They were lucky that they had found him at eighty-seven — a decade earlier he would have known how to deal with the affront. At eighty-seven it simply disheartened him. "They were children," he told me. He fell in readily enough with Diana's suggestion that he and my mother go to Spain.

In January we saw wildflowers in bloom on the borders of the highway that ran along the seacoast, and among them great store of a giant oxalis, almost knee-high, with lovely large yellow flowers. That was most of the pleasure of the visit. There were misunderstandings of the sort only to be enjoyed among close kin. Diana took my part with one trenchant observation. It was not even clear that her speaking up for the fool of the family embittered things further. Perhaps it went unnoticed; in these matters the combatants dwell in different worlds. But the wrangling went on for days, and that was bad for her in her reduced state. She was accustomed to give her opinion, listen carefully to the rejoinder, and if she could not agree, drop the business. How was she to appreciate the high principle of that clan, whose members preferred death to surrender?

She was a creature of the light, still the six-year-old of that bright day when halfway between the goat shed and the silver maples of the ravine where she played alone at building dams on the trickling watercourse, and thinking to go there, she stood still for a moment and looked up at the April sky. "This is happiness" came into her mind, as if in answer to the question she had never consciously asked. When I first knew her, a young woman, she seemed to live under that sign, a joyous temperament. She had it from her mother, who regarded this world as her home, hospitable if you lived in it confidingly. Diana said of her that she could do anything. When we came to move house I discovered that Diana could shift anything—cupboards, chests, wardrobes, and an enormous refrigerator that she teased out of its corner—things that I would call a friend to help me with, though I was a head taller than she and heavier by sixty pounds. When Diana's mother gave her piano to a nephew, I was one of the six men who tailed on to it and sweated and cursed, getting it through the doorway, stumbling with it down the porch steps, stopping twice to catch our breath as we trascined it across the yard, in a final spasm heaving it up onto the flatbed truck. The nephew and his friends clambered up around the piano and were carried away. I was feeling the glow of the successful team effort. When I came into the house again her mother was laughing. She said to Diana, "I brought that thing in here by myself, up the stairs, past the door, and right up against that wall. I don't remember cussing." She gave me a quick glance to see how I was taking it, mischievous but loth to impair my satisfaction.

And now Diana was dismasted, holed between wind and water. She could not bear rebuke directed at anyone. I came to myself at last and would take no provocation. I must have looked hateful all the same. Luckily there had been no compact about the length of our stay. Polite, mournful gestures saw us off.

A HALF-HOUR from Málaga we were flying over the snow-covered high plateau. The roads must have filled with drifted snow; we could not make them out. I do not think we saw a moving vehicle anywhere below us, though from five miles up an auto with snow on its roof would be hardly more conspicuous running than motionless. Every now and then I saw a short straight line traced on the flattened landscape. I asked Diana what she thought the lines might be. She said they must be the dams holding back the water of reservoirs of those mountain lands, iced over now and covered with snow. She had seen the faint depressions behind some of those dams when the airplane had changed course and the pattern of sunlight had altered. The Spaniards have an expression, *la inmensa llanura*, the endless plain, but we were flying over the endless highlands, flattened by snow and distance, shadowless.

Diana was nervous about flying. It was worse this time. We struck what the captain had announced as slight turbulence ahead, and the aircraft fell suddenly some hundreds of feet. The captain ordered us to fasten our seat belts. Diana took my hand. She was watching the starboard wing, which was vibrating as if it might buckle directly. By way of soothing syrup I said, "They're built to stand those stresses." She closed her hand harder on mine. "Please." She knew that I had little imagination and a vapid faith that things would come right. But just then she saw a city beneath us, as if it were rising out of the snow, and there was a cathedral and other towers. "Oh, look." Topography and architecture were potent with her. They drove out fear.

And then lunch appeared, with continued slight turbulence. After a minute or two the captain said, "We have to belay lunch for the time being. Passengers will buckle their seat belts, please. Cabin crew, be seated and buckle up." I said to Diana, "Imagine—he said 'belay.'" "Or just stow it," Diana said. With my habit, my father's habit of glossing life, I said that the captain must have served in the

Navy. "Yes, just stow it." But in a few minutes more we had cleared the zone of slight turbulence. The captain restored lunch, and the cabin crew inquired what the passengers would drink. Wine? A Frenchman across the aisle said under his breath that it would certainly be foul. But I had seen the half-bottles of claret come aboard. I told him the wine was Bordeaux. He said, "My good sir, thank you so much. I can breathe again." I wondered if irony might be contagious, and had he caught it from Diana.

As lunch resolved itself to coffee, still at her porthole she said that we were approaching the Pyrenees. It seemed to me to be too soon for that. I told her that most of the mountain chains of Europe ran west and east, and not north and south like ours. I told her it was just another sierra. I was about to tell her that Europe had fewer plant species than the Americas because of the regrettable disposition of her mountains, which had kept the plants from migrating to the south during the ice ages and north again when the ice receded. But just then several French voices said, "The Pyrenees." Since they were strangers I accepted their decision, but I looked at my watch to see what ailed it. Then I dozed off. When I awakened it seemed that the plane had been losing altitude. We were flying over farmland and villages. Where the hills rose I thought I could see vineyards. "Are those vineyards?" She said they were, and that the hills must be very steep because they were terraced in stone. Terraces . . . I looked at them dreamily and corked off again.

STARING AT THE SUN

I woke once more as I felt her stir beside me. She said, "Look, Paris." I leaned forward to look athwart her. There was an island in the river below, and there was a cathedral on the island, but all that was small, quite small. Clearly, it was a much smaller place than Paris. I said so. She said, "But that's the Ile de la Cité, that's Notre Dame." I said that I had lived in Paris. It was an enormous city. I began to explain that there were a number of towns built on islands in the rivers of France, and a number of them had cathedrals. Then I heard the French passengers say, "Paris, Paris." Diana said, "My navigator." Her eyes were turned to the porthole, looking at the city rising to meet us. She brushed her face with her hand. She was crying quietly.

She had never seen Paris. She had never been in France. The few days we spent in the city were an adventure to her. She had studied French for a year in high school, and been captivated. She told me that she had taken to writing in French, not because it was demanded of her at school but for the pleasure of it. She said she had had the conviction that she could express herself more tellingly in French. French stimulated thought. Writing in French was revelatory, not at all like an exercise. Then her people moved, she changed schools several times, there were no further courses in French. By degrees she left off writing the language, then reading it, and eventually she seemed to have lost it. But she surprised me sometimes with unaccountable flashes. We have a French friend who speaks English with grace and point, and he told us that he had found in an antique shop the frame of an old fireplace, very handsome. There was a chimney, bricked up, in his Paris apartment, and he had exposed the chimney and installed the fireplace there with great satisfaction. He described it to us in detail, and then, affectionately, "You know, it's really quite old, possibly as old as the house. And it's all *en fonte* — how do you say that in English?"

I tried to think of the English equivalent. He tried to think of it. I knew that if the question had not been asked I would have had a better chance at it. Sometimes it is hard to make your tongue call up expressions that are perfectly familiar. You simply can't find them. They won't come. Diana said, "Cast-iron." "Cast-iron, of course," our friend said. "How could it have eluded me?" Well, it had certainly eluded me, but I was used to that. I wondered at her secretly. When I was a boy I had a friend who went to a technical high school, in Brooklyn. In the blacksmith shop he was taught to forge a twentypenny nail by hand, and after that a railroad spike. When he had mastered those things he had to describe the process to the teacher, in French. Coke fire, so many heats (paying attention to color), hammer, tongs, anvil, fullers, upsetting the length of bar steel at one end to make the nailhead, drawing out the point with the hammer, and in the case of the spike, forming a chisel-point — all that in French. Now, Diana had not gone to such a school. Cast-iron.

But why should she weep on seeing Paris from the air? It was not enthusiasm, surely. It was a plaintive something uncharacteristic of her. She had scarcely wept at the death of her mother. She had borne the bromides of the minister's eulogy and listened stonily to his suggestion, "She is not dead, she is just away." When he dismissed the congregation, she was on her feet instantly, calling, "Wait! Please wait." She began to speak, and the hair stood up on the back of my neck for the eloquence of a soul intent on limning another—in the presence of her scandalized kin. It was the one spark of religion struck in that place. If a Kathleen Battle sings "I know that my Redeemer liveth . . . though worms destroy this body, yet in my flesh shall I see God," the proposition *qua* proposition may appear unconvincing. But the unearthly beauty of the performance is itself a promise fulfilled, clearest truth, embodiment of man's hope. Then we drove to the family graveyard. We lowered the coffin into the ground. Diana dropped the first clod upon it and took up a spade to fill in the grave. Embarrassed among her people by their mortal embarrassment—this was just what they had deprecated in Diana's mother—with a kind of fury I did as she did. In the twilight of the raw November day we attacked the mound of heaped earth, shoveling the heavy clay for nearly half an hour before we looked up again and in the falling dark felt rather than saw the morose faces of the family. No, she was not one to weep.

It had started just after the Procedure. I entered the room. Diana was sitting up in bed, leaning towards the young intern who sat on the edge of the bed with her back to me. Diana was talking to her. I knew from the pose of their bodies that they were crying, and quickly I turned and left the room. Diana told me later that the intern had just broken off with the young man to whom she had been engaged. She said, "The poor girl works days and nights at a stretch as they all do, dead for sleep. And now her heart's broken."

That was the first weeping, at the heartbreak that everyone understands if for no better reason than that everyone has been a child, sorrowing. But I was surprised that Diana, talking earnestly to that young woman, wept with her too. A few hours after the Procedure I had been allowed to see her, hitched to electronic devices. She looked ten years younger. A nurse came to give her something—for the pain, as she said gently. Diana thanked her. "The pain is from the surgery. It's nothing to what it was before. I'd rather be alert and know what's going on." That was of a piece with her quiet intransigence. I was glad to have her back.

She was serious about other people's troubles. Her first impulse was to consider how they might be helped, how she might help. Her sympathy was active, it took that form. So there was something that I did not understand when she cried with that unhappy girl. I learned later what it meant, or thought I did. She had been broken. Not by the ten years of pain, not by the diagnostic insouciance of the faculty—"Get married," was one iatric suggestion. "I tried that," she told the physician. "It has not affected my condition." What broke her was the accident that probably saved her life, for there was a time when, not able to stand or sit or lie in bed she seemed to me to be at the point where she might tell me to shoot her. The accident was happening on a doctor who knew his trade. I was reminded how years ago I had had a medical examination because I was on a college sports team. The doctor frowned. "You have an ugly heart murmur. Not good. I'm going to refer you to a cardiac specialist." A Gypsy had told me that I would die before I was thirty, and now I began to be impressed. The cardiac specialist thumped me for a good half hour. "Get dressed." It sounded to me like the Gypsy's death knell. Since the doctor was silent I asked point-blank about my fate. "You're okay." I asked how come the other physician had found an ugly heart murmur. He looked up from his notepad. "Young man, as you go through life you'll discover that most of the world's important work is performed by third-rate people." The explanation was of course luminous. But I could never apply it in practice. Everyone takes the doctor at face value, and the airline pilot who turns out to be a drunk, and the president who turns out to be universally irresponsible. Diana had not believed her various doctors because they all implied that she was a nut case while she was conscious of being quite sane. She was stoical about her physical distress, even at the last when she was in a delirium of pain, and I had assumed, almost, that it was something that could be borne. But when the man who knew his trade found nearly at once what was amiss with her, and explained the dangers of the intervention he proposed, and carried it out successfully, she was for the first time stricken.

DIANA wanted to visit the Louvre. We traversed the long corridor of unremarkable Roman statuary. Since I had no real feeling for the sculpture I looked for dates and attributions. I hardly noticed that we had reached the foot of the grand stairway, and I was startled when she cried out, "Look." I looked, saw again the *Winged Victory* on the landing, surmounting the many steps — saw it with the pleasure that one must feel if only for the remarkable *coup de théâtre.* I turned to say something. She was weeping. I felt sick, as if she had a nervous aberration. It was not enthusiasm. It was more like mourning. It took some time to ascend the staircase, and as we were going upwards she told me, her voice quite steady, that she had seen photographs only, and they conveyed little — weeping the while. We stayed on that landing for nearly an hour, surrounded mostly by family parties of Japanese. Twice while we were there women guides came, the one speaking French to a group of the natives and the other German to her countrymen. I told Diana about the ship-motif of ancient Greek culture to explain the statue's base, and how small ship models had served as a kind of icon in temples and in dwellings. She listened. I told her that Victor Hugo's ode to the fallen Napoleon had a line that must have alluded to the *Winged Victory*, reciting to her the stanza that sums up earthly glory, that speaks of "Victory with flaming wings" and ends "All these fall to us only as the bird alights on the roof." She took it in. She said, "They had more energy than we. Almost every era since ancient times had more energy than ours. The Middle Ages and the great cathedrals. The Renaissance. The fever of the baroque. The ordered delirium of the *Brandenburg* Concertos. Or the nineteenth century—Balzac, Dickens, Tolstoy, Melville. Or Lyell, Darwin, Marx, Freud. Our science is parasitic on the science of the nineteenth century. They simply had more energy." All this, though her face was calm and her tears had stopped, sounded like a dirge. Now, all those things I most powerfully and potently believed. But I had an itch to say that I was living in the twentieth century and had to be getting on with that life, such as it was. Not to be a naysayer but because that was the lament of a broken spirit. Though I knew her to be in other ways indomitable.

Then I remembered that other acute surprise.

But who may abide the day of His coming? For he is like a refiner's fire.

When she came home from the hospital she was under

orders to walk, and as soon as possible to walk four miles a day. In the beginning she could scarcely walk a hundred feet. The stubble was short, but I mowed it down to golf-links standard because she could not negotiate three inches of stubble. A few days later she could walk an eighth of a mile on the flat, and back again until she came to where the path sloped. Going down that easy declivity was hard for her. One day when she had been walking alone she found that she could not go up the slope again. She had to call to me to help her. Then there came the time when she could walk to the great black cherry, just before the path fell away sharply downhill. On a day I was walking to that tree with her, and I was thinking of a captain I had shipped with on the *Nora Mason*, a Dane. I was telling Diana about him, and how, after the battle of Leyte Gulf there was fighting inland, and we were anchored in the roadstead off Tacloban. We had just arrived from Bougainville, carrying troops. When the soldiers had disembarked we anchored in the stream and broke sea watches. In the evening nearly all the ship's officers were on the bridge deck in the mild weather, and we were speculating where we might go next, the captain listening but offering no suggestions. Then we heard artillery. We took little notice, though I remember thinking that it could not be a preparation for an attack, for surely they would not deploy infantry in the jungle at night—such was my naïveté. Suddenly we heard the scream of a shell close aboard, and without stopping to inquire if it was Japanese or friendly fire we ran pell-mell for the shelter of the smokestack. Every man Jack, except the captain. He was still leaning on the rail. The instinctive panic had not affected him. Of course the rest of us saw then that it was childish to imagine that the tin stack could protect us from high explosive. I was telling this to Diana because the incident was characteristic. Captain Nielsen knew that on a ship you could not throw yourself to the steel deck in the hope of avoiding a shell, as if we were infantry in open order, each man looking for a hole. So he had simply not responded to the screech in the air, or else he had governed his nerves not to respond. Some of the men on the bridge deck were older than he, the chief engineer and the second—they had cut and run with the rest of us. And then other things came to me about that skipper. It brought up a voyage that I had forgotten, and I told it to Diana, more or less in order.

THE following day at breakfast the captain said, "Mister, see the motorboat launched. And I'll want you to come along with the stores list." The first man I saw on deck was the bosun. I enlisted him. "Boats, help me pull the cover off the captain's gig." When that was done we hooked the tackles at the boat's bow and stern, and lay in wait for whom we might devour. First we caught the young ordinary from my watch, fresh from the mess, and then an AB. With those reinforcements, hauling on the falls we lifted the boat from its chocks, turned the davits outboard, swung the boat clear of the rail, and lowered away. I asked the bosun if he would come as ballast. He said that he had never been ashore in the Philippines. He thought he would like to get acquainted. I released the AB and simply Shanghaied the boy. Then we put the pilot ladder over the side, and I reported to the captain that the boat was manned and ready.

We tied up to a dock that was newly built, probably by an Army or Navy engineer outfit – the clean timbers shone in the sun. When we scrambled up onto it we remarked a file of soldiers at least a hundred yards in length, and at its head a shack whose planks gleamed like the planking of the dock. The captain turned his head away sharply and a moment later I did too. Behind me the bosun said, "Jesus." The young ordinary asked, "What's that line for?" No one answered. We steered towards the encampment where we would find the officers who might give us our instructions. When we reached it our captain was taken in tow by a colonel and a major who sat him down in an open tent, and we were directed to a warehouse. I asked the supply sergeant there if we could have two coils of three-inch manila. He led us to an array of cordage ranging from small-stuff to great mooring hawsers, all of splendid quality, better than I had seen in any merchant ship. I imagine that all that line must have been made for the Navy, and it seemed to me that I had gained an important insight into how the other half lives. The sergeant was enjoying my surprise. "What we have here is God's plenty." Near the coils of line there was a cask of pelican hooks of an unfamiliar pattern, with a long-tongued camming arm for better leverage and a locking system that looked like business. I cadged a gross of them because our ship carried twenty life rafts on steel racks slung outboard of her bulwarks. The hooks we had on board were short, hard to lock, and given the weight and strain they carried when the vessel rolled in a seaway your hands were in danger during the split second in which you released them. I knew that because the captain had ordered a drill with the newfangled things while we were at sea.

I went down the rest of the list with the sergeant. I had begun to understand that he enjoyed issuing those good things to us, and I felt less apologetic. When we had run through the list, each item checked off, the sergeant said, "How would you like a pair of night glasses? Eight by fifty so you don't have to deal with all that trembling. They pull in all the light there is. They really work." Well, that was certainly a prize. Then he organized the transport to the dock, driving the truck himself while we sauntered after him to put our loot into the boat. We thanked him as he climbed back into the cab, and he waved a magnanimous hand. Then we sat down on the end of the dock, looking seaward at the ship, waiting for the old man.

WHEN we had climbed aboard the *Nora* the captain said, "See the boat secured, Mister. Then come to my cabin." The third mate was on the bridge, looking down at us, and I asked him to take his watch from their housekeeping jobs. By the time the boy had hooked on the tackles in the boat and was on deck again we were four on a side, for that hapless AB had appeared, and we brought the boat up smartly, hand over hand, and drew her aboard to rest in her chocks. I asked the third to unload the boat and see it covered for me. Then I went to the captain. His door was ajar for the sake of the air. I knocked. "Captain." He unshipped the fitting that held the door open, stepped back to let me enter the small cabin, and closed the door after me. He went to the chair at his desk, motioning to me to sit on his bunk. "Make ready for sea. Set sea watches. We shall sail this evening when the tidal stream has turned in our favor. Our orders are for Melbourne. We are to return to this archipelago. Just where will depend on how the fighting goes in these islands. Now, with the troops out of the tweendecks we are somewhat heavily ballasted. I don't like to take a stiff ship into rough seas."

I thought of the rows of three-tiered bunks in the tweendecks. "Sir, would it help if we disassembled the bunks and stowed them on deck? We have the dunnage, and it's only a day's work. Shall I tell Chips to be in readiness tomorrow?"

"That was my first impulse. But I don't want the men to do the work twice."

"Oh, then we'll be carrying troops again?"

"They wouldn't say." He turned and looked out the port,

looked into the brightness. "It's possible that they didn't know. When I pressed them about the nature of the cargo they denied any knowledge of it. I said that we would be sailing to Melbourne in ballast, much of the time in waters famous for heavy weather, with a long fetch of ocean behind the running seas. I said that I must have the vessel in reasonable trim. It was Greek to them. I'm not sure that any of these landsmen know anything at all about the capacity of this ship, whether for troops or freight. And this is wartime. I can remonstrate but I cannot refuse."

That was a long speech for Captain Nielsen. For the most part he kept his uncertainties to himself, and that was a boon to his subordinates. Since as a matter of custom you cannot commune with your captain, and you may make only the most innocuous suggestions, it is better not to know what might be troubling him. He must find his way alone, and generally he does. I imagined that Captain Nielsen saw something beyond a stiff vessel on the run to Melbourne and the inconvenience of carrying troops—though passengers could be dangerous cargo, quite involuntarily. Whatever he saw was not my affair. I admired him, but the punctilio of the sea becomes a habit and makes you incurious in these connections. When he stopped speaking I thought the interview was at an end. "Well, Sir, I'll see to preparing the ship for sea."

"One moment, Mister. On second thought your suggestion is seamanlike. We are lucky to have this crew—quite exceptional—so that I hesitate to give them an extra job. It isn't really sailorizing. There's no satisfaction in it. But the safety of the ship is ultimately their concern. When you muster the men, tell them what we mean to do tomorrow, and tell them the reason."

A few minutes later the crew was assembled just forward of the house. In the captain's name I told them that we were going to Melbourne for orders. A man asked, Would we get shore leave? I thought it likely. Then I told them that we would clean out the tweendecks tomorrow, stowing the steel bunks on deck so as to raise the ship's center of gravity and make her a little more comfortable if we met with heavy weather. Lowering my voice, I gave them an account of how the captain had thought to shift that load topside but had decided that he didn't want to put a good crew to the trouble, since they might have to set up those bunks in the tweendecks once more. And the rest of the story.

"Well, it does sound like troops again," the bosun said. "But the skipper's right. Chips'll have to do his stuff again is all." The carpenter said, "I've been known to do a little work in a good cause." And the ordinary in my watch, a boy from the piney woods of north Georgia who had signed on for his first voyage nearly a year ago when we were in San Diego, a boy green as all verdure: "You can see the captain sets great store by us." He was blushing, but he was pleased to have delivered his sentence among the men. I thought the men were pleased to hear him pronounce their judgment and not be chargeable for the sentiment.

STARING AT THE SUN

I told the bosun to secure the hatches for sea, except for the one forward of the house, number three, through whose hatchway we would haul up the steel bunks the next day, and then to rig the after booms on the mainmast so that we could start the work first thing in the morning. "And you'll secure the watertight doors all through the vessel." I knew I had made a mistake with that last recommendation when he said, "Aye aye, Mister," with a straight face. All-through-the-vessel violated the proprieties. The bosun was thinking that I was too young for my rate, I hadn't learnt manners yet. In my embarrassment I agreed with him. As I went towards the bridge ladder to go up and look about the ship to remind myself of what was to be done, the bosun was telling off two of the nine seamen to go below and tend to the watertight doors. "Let's go forward," he said to the others. By the time I had made my way to the bridge I could hear through the hatchways the clanging of the watertight doors and the groaning of metal on metal as the locking cams were levered into place. Up forward the bosun and his seven seamen had split into twos, two men to a wooden hatch cover, and I heard in the depths of the hold the reverberation of each cover as it dropped into its steel frame. In ten minutes the forward hatch was closed. In five minutes more the heavy tarpaulin had been stretched over the hatch, and the men were securing it, knocking home the wooden wedges with the mallet. "One down!" the bosun cried. The sailors moved aft to the number-two hatch.

When the hatches had been secured and the booms on

the mainmast had been rigged and raised, I sent the men to their dinner. The rest of the day was employed in changing the pelican hooks on the life rafts. It meant clapping a handy-billy on the raft to take the weight, and then easing off the ring that served as a lock for the hook. These were roughly forged, and it took a little doing to slip each ring. The pleasant part was attaching the new hooks that were nicely machined, and hearing them click smoothly as they cammed and locked. We finished the job at sunset. Then sea watches were set. I mustered my own watch, sending one AB forward to make himself useful in picking up the anchor before taking his bow lookout, and the other to his lookout on the wing of the bridge. Our ordinary went to the wheel—the boy from the Georgia hills was a good helmsman, and he was our mud pilot. I called the carpenter to take his anchoring station, and I was about to look for the captain when I saw him leaning on the bridge rail with the third mate at his side. The chief engineer had gotten up steam an hour ago. The ship had swung on its anchor nearly a hundred and eighty degrees as the tidal stream reversed. "Sea watches have been set, sir. The men are standing by on the bow, ready to weigh anchor."

"Lay forward, Mister. Heave up short. The current is heavy. I shall assist you with the engines. Let me know when the brake is off the cable."

I went forward quickly. The carpenter was standing ready with the sledgehammer. When I said, "Back off your brake, Chips," he struck the long brake lever a single blow, and at once I engaged the steam winch. I turned and called to the bridge, "The brake is off, Captain. The winch is heaving." A moment later I heard the bridge telegraph jangle, and the ship began to shudder at the first pounding of the screw. After a minute I looked over the side to see how the chain grew, and I was startled by the speed of the water flowing past the bow. For a moment I wondered if the captain meant to sail out the anchor from its bed. Then I remembered that the stream was running hard and the ship was breasting it. The captain spoke through his megaphone. "How does your cable tend, Mister?" "Nearly up and down, sir." And then, "Up and down, sir." "Heave it home and secure it." When the shank of the anchor was housed snug in the hawsepipe I told the carpenter, "See to your brake, Chips." He struck the brake lever three times with the sledge, and I fixed the claws in position over a link of the heavy cable. I heard the engine telegraph again, and there was a sudden surge. Looking at the water, I knew that the boy at the wheel had responded to the order, "Hard right," for the stream was driving against our port bow. The telegraph jangled again. The ship began to tremble more noticeably. The boy had been ordered, "Midships the helm." It had taken some five seconds to do it, and then the captain had signaled "Full astern." The *Nora* spun round on her keel, and I thought, Now he'll ring "Slow ahead" and he'll tell the boy, "Meet her, handsomely," But no. I was off by twenty seconds or more. The ship was still turning on her keel, and now he gave the order to the helm, and the telegraph clanged "Slow ahead," and then "Half speed," and he must have said to the boy, "Steady as you go." I was not chagrined about my mistaken reckoning—Captain Nielsen was a famous shiphandler, a virtuoso. The stars had brightened. On the wing of the bridge the captain had bent over the pelorus, most likely, and found a star on the heading that he had chosen. The telegraph sounded again. The ship surged forward. He had rung "Full ahead."

In the morning we began to snake out the bunks through the hatchway. The sea was calm, there was no difficulty in using the heavy booms under way. The carpenter, the dayman, and the ordinary in the second mate's watch cribbed the stuff securely against the bulwarks port and starboard, using the dunnage that had come with the cots when we first took them aboard, and some planks from the carpenter's personal cache. After him the third mate would be on duty, twelve to four, and his ordinary would serve as helper to the carpenter and the dayman. Then it would be my turn, four to eight, and the ordinary in my watch would hold the lengths of dunnage for them to nail in place, if necessary until the light failed. As it happened, the job was finished before five in the afternoon. Just at five the Navy gun crew stood to their 20-millimeter guns, and toy balloons went up for them to shoot at. The tracer shells made the stream of fire visible so that the gunners did not use the gunsights but aimed more conveniently by adjusting the direction of the stream, flowing as if from a high-pressure hose. Only one of the dozen balloons escaped with its life. It was in some sense reassuring to know that we were not entirely helpless, though steaming alone without the protection of a convoy's collective battery. But the truth was that an attack from the air would be sudden, and the marksmanship of our gunners would play a small part in our chances of getting away with it. As for the errant submarine, during an evening or morning twilight she would find us long before we had picked up her periscope wake, even with our splendid new glasses. The three point fifty cannon in the gun tub on the stern would be a talisman only, as we had learned in the Atlantic, and would sink with the ship. But no one on the *Nora* was much preoccupied with that.

The passage was uneventful, except for the two-day blow when we were some seven hundred miles from Melbourne. In the worst of it we managed to keep steerageway, going at half speed or slow. Shifting the bunks topside had eased the vessel enough so that we did not take too much of a pounding, though she was very wet on deck. A dollop of sea would come over the bulwarks and she would hang on the body of the wave, rolling under the load, but she would right herself when she sank into the trough, the water pouring out through the scuppers. A messman with a bucket of slops to throw overboard was caught by a green sea and slung into a corner of the deckhouse—better than going overboard. Somehow he had clung to his bucket, and for days he had to bear witty remarks as well as his bruises. The gale was lusty enough to keep the watch officer and the lookout inside the bridge, watching the helmsman and the standard compass, for there was little to be made out beyond the windows, covered in sheets of spray. Since we had plenty of searoom, the blow was more nuisance than hardship. The greatest danger was remote, though it happens all over the watery world: collision with another ship under way or with a floating derelict. The wind and sea would not permit us to maneuver smartly even if we saw the steaming vessel or the hulk, so there was little to be done about that. Naturally the men damned the noise of the wind and the *Nora*'s pitching and rolling. But they waited patiently enough for the gale to abate. Captain Nielsen was on the bridge for two days and nights, resting in a canvas deck chair when the ship's motion allowed it. He was the man in charge.

Two days later, shortly after daybreak we made our landfall. We hoisted the pilot flag as we stood in towards the city. While steaming in the roadstead we were met by a motor launch that was being tossed about in the swell. We turned to give the little craft a lee and slowed for her to come alongside. We were expecting the pilot and we had let down not the awkward accommodation ladder—in this sea it could easily be smashed, especially its landing stage—but the supple, rope-jointed pilot ladder. The pilot appeared on the deck of the launch. As the boat rose on a wave he jumped and seized a rung above his head, swung till he found his footing, then swarmed up the ladder. I greeted him as he came aboard and I shook his hand. I was about to conduct him to the bridge when I heard a shout from below. The pilot said, "That'll be your Army chaps." I looked over the side. There were two American officers on the deck of the launch, their upturned faces looking at once helpless and aggrieved. I certainly had not seen them on the deck of the little craft while the pilot was climbing to our bulwarks. I thought, Are there always two of them? But it was clear that they could not perform the pilot's athletic feat. It was simply their misfortune not to be seamen. So I raised my hand to suggest that they wait a bit. They were not pleased, the launch was bobbing and plunging, but I could not still the waters for them. I told the AB who had lowered the ladder with me to take the pilot to the captain, and then to ask if we might stop engines because two Army officers wanted to come on board. In a short time the ship lost its way. The launch closed with us again, and the two officers scrambled up creditably.

I shook hands with each of them. One was a major, the other a captain. Both wore the insignia of the Transportation Corps. I said, "I would like to take you to the master"—instinctively I avoided the word "captain" because those two were on an official mission, and I wanted them to understand that no mere captain but a great personage was in command of the *Nora Mason*. "I would like to take you to the master, but right now he's conferring with the pilot." The major was about to say something when the ship's engines went ahead again—wonderful thing about steam and reciprocating engines, you don't require a clutch mechanism and you have full pressure always for any speed. Seeing him slightly disconcerted I explained that the pilot would be telling the master where we would anchor or dock, and how he proposed to get us there, since every order he gave the man at the wheel and every signal on the engine telegraph was by the master's leave, for he was in command of the ship and he must be satisfied with the pilot's plan and then with his every action in carrying it out. Since they were discussing matters that had to do with the safety of the ship I could not take it upon myself to disturb them. I was on duty myself, and I would not be able to take them to the master until I had seen the anchor down and set, or the ship riding to a mooring buoy or at a dock, since I had responsibility for those things—under the master. And he would be calling me, at his convenience, to have all three deck officers take their stations for anchoring or for tying up.

I tried to be at once sublime and endearing as I delivered this. When it was over the major said, somewhat acidly—for there was acid in his brevity—"You're going to a dock."

"In that case I am certain, Major, that the pilot has so informed the master."

The major said, "You are going to a dock that I have designated."

"That's very good of you, Major. And I am sure that the choice is an appropriate one. But it is the master of the *Nora Mason* who judges what is appropriate for the vessel under his command."

"Young man, would you mind telling me how old you are?"

"Major, I am old enough to have the berth of first officer of this ship, under a master who is a thorough seaman — his license reads extra master mariner, any tonnage, any waters. And he engaged me to be the first mate of this vessel, the master's deputy and executive officer. I have a master's license myself, and the courtesy title in wartime of Lieutenant Commander in the Naval Reserve, a title, I imagine, that is comparable to a majority in the United States Army."

"We have to see your master before this ship docks."

"That is not possible, Major. You are asking for an interview with the captain of an aircraft in his cockpit as he is preparing to land. You must understand that your claim is secondary to that of the safety of this ship."

I was holding up my end, fighting my corner, probably at the expense of the captain I wanted to protect, but I did not know that and I was quite pleased with myself. Imagine that fellow asking how old I was! I had wrung more salt water out of my socks than he had sailed over yet, and he wanted to lay down the law on the *Nora.* The only good thing I could say for him was that he had been called to an honorable estate: Stendhal had served in the transportation corps or commissariat, and had behaved with great gallantry in the retreat from Moscow; it was possible that this pushy reserve officer might be a brave man in a trial. I was saved from hopelessly compromising Captain Nielsen because he appeared at the canvas dodger on the bridge, and called out, "Mister, docking stations. Tell the second and third mates that the wind is blowing onshore at force five, and we shall approach the dock with caution."

"Aye aye, Sir." And to the two officers, "You'll excuse me, gentlemen."

"Before you go, what are all these beds doing here?"

I explained hurriedly that we had brought them up from the tweendecks so as to ease the vessel in rough weather.

"I see."

His question seemed to me to be pointless, and I went on about my business.

THE captain told me later that the officers had decreed that no one from the ship might go ashore. No one was to come on board—unless he had a pass. We would be loading ammunition. The captain had pointed out that the longshoremen would be coming and going, and if there was concern about secrecy, it was hopeless. They said that the longshoremen would be American soldiers.

"I forbore to tell them that American soldiers drank beer and spirits like other people. In any case, something is quite odd here."

The captain handed me a list of the munitions to be loaded, itemized on three pages. From the weights given I estimated that we would have to discharge some two-thirds of our ballast of coral sand. "We'll need clamshell hoists to shift the sand, Captain."

He had mentioned that to them. They had promised to have the clamshell hoists at the dockside tomorrow morning, and trucks to haul the sand away. Then he said, "I asked them if the crates and cases were marked on the outside as usual. The major said yes, they were all stenciled with the type, batch number, and so on." I said, "If those goods are paraded through the port there won't be much secrecy." "Yes. Something is odd here."

We were two days discharging ballast, since it was carried off by too small a relay of trucks. We were nearly two days loading ammunition for the same reason. On the following day the major and the captain came aboard to tell us that we were not to sail but must stand by for further orders. I was surprised that the captain made no observation about it after we had heard what they had to say. We waited four days. Then we had another military visit. We were to set up the bunks again in the tweendecks. I was present when Captain Nielsen got the news — I think that at this point the captain wanted a witness to our negotiations with the Army.

The captain said, "Major, carrying passengers and explosives is forbidden everywhere in the world by international conventions." The major said, "Captain, this is wartime. These are orders." Captain Nielsen said, "I assume that ignorance in high places is at the origin of this irresponsible dictate." The major hesitated. "I did not formulate the orders but I am under instructions to deliver them to you and to see them carried out."

"Mister Mate, call the radioman to me. Have him bring a notebook." "Yes, Sir." We were in a corner of the bridge, and I had to make my way past the officers and Captain Nielsen, so that I heard, "Major, I am afraid that I must embarrass you. I shall register a written protest to whom it may concern. I trust that you will deliver that protest to your superiors."

I went down the bridge ladder to the radio shack. Sparks was seated with his feet on the desk, wearing his headphones. He had to monitor radio traffic although we were forbidden to contribute to it. While monitoring he was reading a book, after the manner of his kind. I used to take every occasion to twit him about his thirst for knowledge, but this time I was disturbed by what the officers had told us, and how the captain had taken it. Left to myself I would have shrugged—actually, I felt immortal, actually. But the captain had made a convert of me. It did not occur to me to flee that pest-ship, get myself into sick bay in Melbourne—I had two tropical diseases—and look out for a vessel that would not be the subject of an insurance claim. On the contrary I fell in with the captain's attitude, espousing it for its ghostly honor.

> I 'listed at home for a lancer,
> *Oh who would not sleep with the brave?*
> I 'listed at home for a lancer,
> To ride on a horse to my grave.

Long ago I had read that warning notice, which was in fact an incitement, a seduction. When I got to go ashore for good I began to imagine that every landsman's occupation was inglorious, and all trades, their gear, and tackle, and trim. For me it was the expulsion from the Garden, where I had lived immured with much content and the happy prospect of drowning if my luck held. Captain Nielsen was certainly disabled from seeing things aright. Besides being a damned foreigner he was romantic, just the man to go down with the ship. This was the first time since I had sailed with him that I looked upon him as a resident alien.

> For round me the men will be lying
> That learned me the way to behave,
> And showed me my business of dying:
> *Oh who would not sleep with the brave?*

The irony of the verse (Housman out of Heine, from a fine old stable) was patent to me. I could read English. But servitude voluntarily embraced was a heady absinthe. I said,

"Sparks, the captain wants you on the bridge with your notepad. You'll take down what he says, and I'm sure he'll want you to type it up right away so that he can give a copy to those Army officers." He took off his headset, picked up a pad, and climbed the bridge ladder before me. When he was in the bridgehouse he said, "Good morning, Captain," and sat down at the chart table. The captain spoke as if he were reading aloud from a written text. I thought, These foreigners. He said that his protest would be entered in the ship's log, and that he would dispatch a copy by mail to the owners, whom he trusted would bring the matter to the attention of their senators and their representatives in Congress, to the secretary of the army, and to the secretary of state. He recited, "This ship, laden with explosives, and carrying no passengers, risks the lives of thirty-one seamen in case of accident or enemy action. Every member of the crew of the *Nora Mason* understands that perfectly — it is his calling. With passengers, if the ship blows up, the toll will be in the hundreds, and the victims will die ignorant and unprepared. I regard these instructions as unlawful and unconscionable." He said, "Sparks, put that in typescript, in four copies. And bring me the original for these gentlemen." Sparks went off, and I heard him tumble down the ladder. The captain said, "Now, I am being forced to carry out orders that are wantonly careless of men's lives. I know very well that if I were to resign my command in protest you would find a substitute, if necessary from the offscourings of the Melbourne or Sydney docks. I am responsible for this ship and for the lives of her men. I will not quit my post because I cannot assume that my successor will be sufficiently mindful of his responsibilities. It will take two days or more to set up the bunks in a single hold. The soldiers will be miserably cramped. But I must see to it that in case of mischance they will be concentrated in one part of the vessel and can be evacuated swiftly. If I were in your place I would make the strongest representations that this disastrous business be canceled. The *Nora Mason* is an enormous bomb, and you are sending me some hundreds of soldiers to blow up with the ship. Major, you are I believe what is called in the United States Army a field-grade officer, and you, Captain, are reckoned an officer and a gentleman. In your place, no matter what embarrassment I might expect, I would not have it on my conscience that I transmitted orders like these and said nothing to my superiors about the possible consequences."

The major said nothing. The captain said nothing.

Captain Nielsen said, "Very well." He turned to me. "Mister, when the radioman brings that document you'll give it to these gentlemen and you'll escort them to the gangplank." And he left the bridge.

We assembled the bunks in the tweendecks, in the hold just abaft the house. Then we waited three days. By this time the men had been driven, as Mark Twain put it in his dealings with The Hartford Light and Power Company, to the verge of irritation. Three delegates, three senior seamen, the bosun, the carpenter, the watertender waited on me to lodge a protest in the name of the crew about those long days of quarantine. They wanted shore leave. They would be reasonable. They would go ashore in shifts. I informed them that if they went to the captain in a body of three it would be called mutiny as a matter of admiralty law. They did not appreciate the joke. I told them that the captain was under orders. "You know he filed a formal protest. You know he hopes the Army will change its mind about troops plus explosives. Every day that passes makes that chance more likely." Then the bosun surprised me. "The captain's thinking about the troops. Why isn't he thinking about the crew? We'd like to go ashore before we shove off again in this hooker to go up or down with her."

"Boats! The captain can't give you permission to do that. This is wartime. He has his orders. If you're so eager why don't you take French leave? The gangplank's right there for you."

"Very funny. As if there's a man aboard this floating coffin who would do that. I knew it was a big mistake to come to you for help." He walked away. The other two were looking at me. "Well, what did you expect me to say?"

The watertender said, "We thought you might say something intelligent. Something we could tell the men so they'd think you were on their side. Instead you talk like a company man."

FIVE days passed, and the tension fell. Two companies of the Philippine Scouts came on board with their field packs and their weapons. Trim, quiet men. They disposed their gear below and bolted up again to the deck. Confinement down there did not agree with them. Since they were pleasant and somewhat retiring they were the more exotic and the more welcome to the crew. I was on the bridge when they lined up on the deck below me for chow—a mess tin of rice decorated with a dab of canned salmon. The sight and smell of that grain were too much for me. I borrowed a plate from the galley, went to the tail of the line, and begged a portion. The corporal in charge was gracious about my gratitude. He explained that the dish was their staple ration. Now, that plain boiled rice was not exactly what I had been raised on, but still it brought up mother, home, and beauty bright. I planned to have a helping daily. It was food with some life to it, far beyond canned vegetables and the beef that had matured for at least a year in the ship's freezer and crumbled when the fork touched it. The Philippine Scouts were aces with me.

NOWADAYS merchant ships are containerized, computerized, and a little smaller than Long Island. Navigation is much dependent on electronics. In my time the captain and the three mates did the navigating by hand. Each of the three deck officers also had his specialty that by custom assigned him his particular duties. The first mate was the housekeeper, with a notebook always in his pistol pocket for recording the endless jobs that have to be done and done over. The second was the navigation officer *par excellence* — he wound the chronometers every day and wrote down their daily error, plus or minus, as measured against the time tick broadcast by radio. He posted the Notices to Mariners that described changes in charts, the position of landmarks and seamarks, the altered characteristics of lights and buoys, and the position of new-minted dangers to navigation. I used to think it arbitrary that he was also the ship's doctor, so much cerebration having been imposed on him already. The third took his place at the engine telegraph when the vessel was maneuvering and the captain or the pilot had to look sharp from the bridge. For the rest he was on his best behavior. I sailed once with a young fellow who had been third mate on a three-island ship running coastwise from Boston to the Gulf ports — New York, Baltimore, Savannah, Jacksonville, Tampa, and points west to Texas. After a year of that he remembered his early religious training and went to confession. He told me it took a long time. The priest heard him out. Then, after a long moment, "Well, son, you've never made a graven image, have you?"

All these arrangements worked well enough in the Pleistocene, provided that the skipper was decent and knew his trade. By decent I mean effective. Many a decent captain was slightly cracked, or at least eccentric. I shipped with one who had a severe migraine headache as soon as he boarded his vessel, was in dreadful misery during the passage, and was cured when he stepped ashore. He loved ships—and what could a seaman hope to do ashore? Some were embittered, some were mean, some had a nasty temper. But generalship was their forte, the essential gift being unfailing inspiration. They might be careful men, they might be full of dash. Each of them had the eye that sizes up a situation at once—and then he listened with delight to the appropriate orders issuing from his mouth. When you have been long in the society of absolute monarchs you find that something of the tyrant has been communicated to you. Some years ago, hopelessly landlocked, I got into an elevator on the ground floor of a tall office building. The elevator was very nearly full, and as I stepped aboard it sank two inches. I didn't like that, but now the doors had closed, and the machine was hauling us up. At the next stop there were a man and a woman waiting to rise in the world. After an instant's hesitation because the car was full, they bulled their way in—that's what the middle class does anymore, making me pine for a hereditary aristocracy. At once the elevator sank about two feet. The doors closed. I pressed the button for the very next stop, towards which the car was lumbering uncertainly. When the doors opened I bundled the pair out and left the elevator myself. I explained the tactic while ringing for the next elevator. After a bit the male member began to mumble about my performance, first to the air and then to his wife, because no cars had stopped for him. I said, "Didn't you see that the car fell a couple of feet when you got aboard?" That was unfair. Of course he had seen nothing. He had been intent on his bourgeois purposes. "If you don't care about your life that's fine with me. But won't you have a care for this unfortunate lady?" He opened his mouth to speak, and I said, "Silence below decks, you accomplished idiot." Thereupon he grew calm, not because he had been struck by my reasoning but because of the tone of command. I don't go through life making observations of that kind to strangers. I am reserved, not to say diffident, not to say shy. But my half-crazed captains had come alive in me when I felt the ship beginning to founder.

At sea life was boring and full of interest. For one thing you lived out in the weather, and that was ever changing. I remember seeing whales for the first time in the great deeps off the coast of Peru. Every man not in shackles tumbled up on deck to watch the lazy grace of the huge beasts, spouting steam and seawater. An odor came to us like the fresh herb-smell of grayling. The sailors were excited as children — the man at the wheel did the unthinkable, dashing to a port for a look and dashing back to his duty, in the presence of the mate, who was free himself to watch the great fish and understood the helmsman's temporary insanity and escapade.

We shaped a course east of the Torres Strait, paralleled the eastern coast of New Guinea a hundred miles off, and then steered north to approach the Philippines. On one fresh, calm day, my fellow officers and the captain on the bridge, I took the noon sight with them to give us our latitude (the sun was almost directly overhead), and the second mate set down the captain's position on the passage chart as usual. The ceremony accomplished, I was officially off duty. I went below to my cabin, took off my shoes, and lay down on my bunk clothes and all for a nap. I fell asleep almost at once. At about 12:30 p.m. a bomber came down out of the sun. No one noticed it since no one was still looking up in that direction through the shaded lens of the sextant. The scream of the bomb came before the sound of the aircraft. I did not hear it. What I heard in my bunk was an explosion. It convinced me that the three-inch fifty at the stern had fired off a round, and I knew that no gunnery practice had been scheduled. I laced my shoes to go on deck and turn aft, but when I came through the companionway I saw a column of smoke rising from the number-three hatch. The bomb had gone through one of the hatch covers on the port side of the hold. Then, to my astonishment, I heard the long baleful hootings of the steam whistle that signaled abandon ship. I ran to the bridge ladder to get my orders from the captain, and only when I looked down from the ladder did I see that the vessel had lost way completely. The captain said that the engines had failed in an instant, and the important thing was to muster the soldiers and release the life rafts and the cargo nets.

We got those things done swiftly, almost as in a dream. I remember telling the captain in charge of the Scouts that the soldiers must drop their packs, stack their rifles on the deck, and climb down into the rafts by the cargo nets. He said that he could not allow Army property to be left behind, he was responsible for every pair of boots, and so forth and so on to the tune of "Garryowen." It did not strike me how like it was to the speech with which I had entertained the Army officers in Melbourne. "Captain, the man who commands this vessel has given the signal to abandon ship. You are wasting time when every second counts. And you may not carry your duffel into the life rafts." In fact, I had no pressing sense that every second counted. I was benumbed by the expectation that the ammunition would go off in a moment. I was going about my business quite mechanically. "I take it that your men are all present? See them disembarked. You must be the last of your unit to leave the ship. After that the ship's officers will go into the boats." As I spoke I took the rifle from the nearest soldier. I set the piece butt down on the steel deck and invited the next two soldiers to stack their weapons with the one I held. When I saw the rest of the men following suit I told the captain to order them to drop their packs where they stood. I moved away before he could argue further. Captain Nielsen called from the bridge. "See the boats lowered, Mister." "Yes, Sir." As I turned to see it done I found that the bosun, who was starboard stroke in our double-banked boat, was lowering away with the crew assigned to her—my watch and men from the engine room. Aft on the same side the captain's motorboat was being launched by its crew. I moved aside to see up forward beyond the plume of smoke. The third mate was alone on deck on the port side, showing that his boat was in the water and already manned. That was smart work. Then I went round the house, looking aft to the second mate's boat station. Something had kinked in the after falls. A sailor sprang to catch two lines of the fourfold fall and delivered a splendid kick. It was below my line of sight but I knew it had been effective because the second and his men were slacking away while the hero was riding down the fall to be the first man in the boat. I thought I must find out who that was. A few moments later the captain ordered me away. As I straddled the rail to find footing on the cargo net I looked up at the bridge and was relieved to see that he was coming down the bridge ladder. He was moving with all deliberate speed. For a moment I wondered if he too was proceeding on automatic pilot. Then it came to me that his steady demeanor was a habit, and if he were to hurry he might provoke panic. The carpenter was waiting for him at the motorboat. Captain Nielsen ordered him down. When the carpenter was over the side on the cargo net the captain straddled the rail, looked up and down the decks, and descended. From my place in the stern sheets of the number-one boat I turned to see him go aboard his gig. At once he began to take the starboard side rafts in tow. He called to me. "Mister, go around to the port side, and have your three boats take a line to each of the rafts. Tow them to windward and follow me. When we are at a reasonable distance we'll slip our towline and come back to give you a hand."

There was no more than a ripple on the sea's face, but the light airs were moving the ship, and we had to pull with a will, hand over hand, to get up enough speed to pass her bow. As we did that we found that the two boats had taken the rafts in tow without being ordered to do so—smart work again. We pulled past them after tossing them the end of our long sea-painter to make fast in the lead boat. That done, I looked round for the captain's flotilla. He was nearly a quarter of a mile away to windward, hauling ten life rafts along. Our own three boats' crews fell into stroke together. I was surprised that after a dozen strokes—with the burden of the unwieldy oblong rafts, the legs of the passengers immersed in the water, and their feet bearing on the netting that served as a bottom to keep each man in place like a half-tide rock—we were walking away with them, handily. In fifteen minutes the captain halted, slipped his towline, and headed back for us. In a short time he had us in tow. I had to look to my steering oar so that the boats would not take a sheer or cumber one another. But I turned quickly to look at the ship. Her high bow acted as a sail even in the near calm. Her stern was all I could see of her. After I had turned back to tend the steering oar it came to me that no smoke was rising from the *Nora.*

When we had reached the other rafts and had bent our lines to theirs, the captain said, "Come alongside, Mister." I told my crew that we would approach the motorboat to leeward, and the port side must stand by ready to toss oars when we were close aboard.

The captain said, "At the moment there's no sign of fire that I can see. What do you make of it?" "Sir, I took one quick look at her only. But I did not see smoke."

He turned to the *Nora.* Then, "Bosun, you had more opportunity to watch the ship. Did you see smoke?"

"No, Captain, I didn't. I wondered if the breeze had freshened where the *Nora* is. I thought the wind might be blowing the smoke forward, hidden by the hull and the house. But I couldn't see any rippling in the water at the stern. Of course we might have been too far off for me to see that."

The captain nodded. "We'll jill about for a little. We seem to be drifting at nearly the same speed as the ship."

After a quarter of an hour the captain said, "Mister, I want you here in the stern sheets with me. Boats, take charge of the steering sweep and bring the mate to me."

The bosun pulled in his oar and we changed places. When I had shipped his oar again he said, "Give way together." It was a matter of a few feet but I pulled to avoid being struck by the man forward of me in the boat. And the oarsmen set me alongside the motorboat at the stern sheets. The captain moved to the port side with the tiller still under his arm. "Sit beside me."

After a moment he said in a low voice, "This is ideal weather for abandoning ship. The trouble is that the men in the rafts are up to their waists in seawater. They'll be pretty well marinated by sunset. Another day and they'll be in serious trouble. We can take twenty more in the boats, in relays. And the crew will have to take their turn in the rafts. As we weaken from exposure our strength will fail so that we'll not be fit for any exertion that might make a difference. I expect that you've been considering these things."

"Yes, Sir. But I was thinking most about the fresh-water ration."

"Quite."

He was silent.

"Mister, I'm going to send you off to the *Nora*, to board her and reconnoiter. Of course I want you to board her alone."

"Yes, Sir."

"Be as careful as you can. I depend on you to tell me what condition the ship is in. I would advise that you try the number-four hatch first, since it is open."

"Yes, Sir."

"How did the men behave in the boats?"

"Well, Captain, the third mate was the first to launch and man his boat. The second was a bit later because there was a kink in the fall. One of his men kicked it free while it was under load. By the time my boat had come round the *Nora*'s stem both their boats had taken the port-side rafts in tow. And you know, Sir, the bosun's a seaman. He's always steady. He steadies me."

"Good. We have an unusual crew. Now, when you board the *Nora* look around you. If there are signs of danger be particularly cautious. In any case, tell the bosun to stand off, at least two cable lengths."

"Yes, Sir."

"You follow me?"

"Yes, Captain."

"Very well. Take command of your boat, Mister. And good luck."

My boat. Well, a lifeboat is no racer. It carries a good deal of stuff for flotation to keep it from sinking if it is swamped, and its lines are developed to make it somewhat less likely to capsize than, say, a whaleboat. But it is no thing of beauty. And I had pulled in whaleboats. That left me, where lifeboats were concerned, with the affection you feel for the runt of the litter or the spoiled second son. They do their job – but they are not good pulling boats. I could see after every dozen strokes that we were gaining on the *Nora*, but it was slow work; perhaps we were making two knots. I remembered that I ought to be grateful that there was no sea running. However, I was impatient to board the ship. Some lines came to me, lines from a poem of my shipmate Juan Soto, after Rilke—because he was an autodidact he was obliged to borrow from the best sources only—that I had turned into English for him, since he meant to be not a Spanish poet only but ecumenical, like Rubén Darío, and that poem ended like this:

> Airs that stirred in spring the starflower,
> The rose mallow in high summer.

Juan Soto had a spark. I decided that I was in fact grateful, but let me board the *Nora.* And after a half hour I said, "Port side, toss oars," and we were alongside. I scrambled up the cargo net and put a leg over the rail. No smoke was rising from the hole in the hatch cover. I told that to the men. Then I said, "Boats, pull away two cable lengths." He said, "That's all right. We're in a good berth here." I was taken aback. When I did not answer, he said, "It's all right. We talked about it."

That damned sea lawyer. I said, "That's the captain's orders. Port side, shove off. Oars. Give way together." And as they pulled away, "Two cable lengths, Bosun."

I slid off the rail and passed along the house towards the number-four hatch. As I went by the corner I was startled to see the stacked rifles standing sentry, and the packs neatly drawn up by each stack. Instinctively I raised my eyes looking for tents and men—the scene was so like a bivouac on the naked plain of the deck. I threaded my way among the gear and the weapons to the coaming of the open hatch, and I peeked bashfully down the column of sunlight into the hold. The three-tiered bunks were made up as for an inspection. It was worse than the stacked rifles, all those taut blankets turned down with hospital corners in the city of the dead. I tried to hearten myself with the kid joke, "What'd you expect, ostrich plumes?" If the *Nora* went down she would go down shipshape. On the ladder I missed my footing and swore. There, that was better. I walked to the far tier of bunks on the port side where the light was dim and went forward towards the steel bulkhead to find the watertight door, stepping with care over the doubled plates welded to the deck at the foot of the I-beams that stiffened the strakes of the hull. A fellow could take a nasty fall here. By the time I reached the forward bulkhead my eyes could make things out in what had been increasing darkness. I found the levers on the door easily, top and bottom, and wrenched them free of the wards. The door opened to electric light in the port-side gangway that ran under the house to the number-three hold. Shucks, I should have tried the switch in number four. As I came up to the bulkhead I felt a flush of heat. At first I thought it was internal. I clucked impatiently. But in a moment I understood that the heat was coming from the steel bulkhead. I touched it tentatively. The levers on the watertight door would be too hot to grasp barehanded. I thought about my bandanna handkerchief, and then something better occurred to me. I was wearing a T-shirt. I peeled it off, wrapped it around the lower lever. It took a hard pull because the metal had expanded in the heat. The upper one was more stubborn still. I supposed I would have to go topside to one of the deck lockers for a singlejack or a mallet. But I was loth to make another trip. I attacked the lever again, and it slipped about an inch. Perhaps I had not given it my best shot because I did not know what might be doing on the other side of the door. But now I heaved at it with all my weight. The lever turned. I staggered back, holding it swaddled in my shirt. A jet of steam came past the half-opened door, catching most of my left arm and the left half of my chest. I felt very little of that, but then I stepped back prudently, waiting for the steam to dissipate. It smelled of scorched things. I wondered if the steam-smothering system had turned on because of the heat generated by whatever had been burning. After a while I reached through the door on the other face of the bulkhead, groping for the light switch. I pressed it, but there my luck ended. No lights came on. I had to find a flashlight or a lantern, so I retraced my steps along the lighted passageway under the house, turned on the lights in the number-four hold, making my way much more quickly on this return journey. When I was on the main deck again I thought that the only place where I was sure to find a flashlight was my cabin. When I got there I could find nothing. I went out through the companionway, and ran up the bridge ladder on the port side. Near the chart table there was a four-cell flashlight hanging on a post that supported the carline; a broad leather band made a kind of holster for it. I lifted it from its place, pushed the switch forward. It was working.

When I got back to number three the bulkhead seemed hot as ever, but there was no further discharge of steam. Now I could see the sunrays coming through the hole in the hatch cover. The sunlight was focused on charred pieces of dunnage that held down a wooden case containing small arms ammunition, also charred but not consumed. I tried to find evidence of the explosion—certainly I had heard one. But the flashlight beam showed me nothing to the purpose. Turning the light here and there, I saw a three-inch pipe at deck level that had burst or been shattered and was leaking water. It was a steam line, certainly, and I knew where it led, branching up to the main deck to serve the windlasses at each mast and the capstan on the bow. That was the only discovery I made with the flashlight. I imagined that the bomb must have been more or less a dud—capable of a bit of spiteful damage but for the rest a failure. I saw no other signs of fire anywhere else in the hold. I must go back to tell the captain.

When I emerged from the hatch I went towards the starboard bulwarks, looking where I might expect to see the number-one boat. Puzzled by its absence I turned and looked aft over the water. The captain's flotilla was nearly dead astern, perhaps a mile and a half away. I thought to go to the port side, but just then I heard a voice. I leaned over the rail. The boat was lying by the cargo net. The bow oarsman on the starboard side had his arm through the mesh, and the stern was angled off thirty degrees or so. The bosun was standing up in the stern sheets with the sweep under his arm. I looked down at the mutineers, annoyed and touched by their conduct. After a moment I said, conversationally, "Boat ahoy." Eight faces looked up at me. The bosun leaned against his sweep and the boat came in parallel to the cargo net. I went down into the boat and took the oar from him. He went to his bench. We shoved off. On our way to the skipper I told the men what I had seen. One asked if there wasn't a sign of that bomb, because it might be ticking away. I said that I had not seen any debris that looked like fragments of metal, and certainly nothing that looked like a bomb, in working order or not. But with no more illumination than a flashlight it was hard to search every corner. And I began to doubt that I had done the right thing in leaving the ship. The bosun said, "Your arm and chest don't look good." I inspected myself and was surprised at what I saw. The bosun said, "You don't want to have the sun on that." He boated his oar and unbuttoned his chambray shirt. He reached it to me. Holding the steering oar with my legs, I got into it dutifully. "Thank you. I don't feel anything yet." "It doesn't look good. It'll bother you in a while." Just a few minutes later I had the shivers, my teeth began to chatter. I still felt no pain, even when the shirt rubbed as I moved the sweep. I thought it strange that the body would react in that way. I wondered if I had been afraid. Then I felt feverish. "Boats, I have to sit down. Can you change with me? I can pull but I have to sit." He told me to sit down where I was, he would take my oar. And he boated his own. I made an attempt at dissuading him. He said, "You have to report to the old man, and you've got fever and chills. Save your strength to make your report."

Captain Nielsen must have seen that something was amiss in our boat a quarter of a mile off. He said nothing as we drew close aboard. The bosun grasped the gunwale of the motorboat. He said quietly, "The mate has been scalded, Captain. He has a spell of fever just now." The captain nodded. "I see. Can you come aboard, Mister?" "Certainly, Sir." "Good. Bosun, take your boat to relieve the second officer. Tell him to come to me."

I got into the motorboat and sat down as before in the stern sheets. I felt giddy. I managed to tell him what I had found on the *Nora*, and what I had not found. I told him of the ruptured pipe that might have smothered the fire. I said I had not been able to make out if the steam-smothering apparatus had worked at all. I said that I had found no debris except for the scorched dunnage and the scorched small arms ammunition box. As for the steam itself, once the hold had been vented by the open door it was hot but bearable in there — one could look about and examine things.

When the second brought his boat alongside the captain told him that he wanted a reconnaissance in force. "Your ordinary will be boat keeper. Take all the lights you can find — the electricity isn't functioning in the number-three hold — and go over everything carefully. If things look safe to you, go to the bridge for the semaphore flags and wigwag to me. If you're not sure of what you find, don't hesitate to come back and report."

The chief engineer was in the captain's boat. He said that he ought to be one of the party. "I want to look at that pipe, Captain." The second took him off and told his oarsmen to give way.

In what seemed about three-quarters of an hour after the second mate and his crew had boarded the ship — during which time I was not of much use to myself or to others — the captain said, "There's the second now." The man on the bridge held out his flags at the horizontal, to left and right: the sign for the letter *R* and the sign for attention. Then he sent: "The chief thinks all danger of fire is over. The broken pipe can be replaced to restore steam pressure."

By way of answer, the captain called out to the bosun and the third mate to stand by for towing. When the rafts were unscrambled the motorboat took the whole flotilla in tow. I am uncertain about that leg of the passage, but I remember being helped up the cargo net. The next thing that I was conscious of was that I was in my bunk and had been sleeping. I fell asleep again. When I awoke the *Nora* was under way. It was dawning. At that hour someone else was standing my watch, and I did not care.

THESE things I told Diana in the fall of the year when she was learning to walk again, and we walked together to the big cherry tree. I left out details that were not to my purpose on that day, for I meant to be telling her about Captain Nielsen, the foreigner whom I much admired.

Two days after we had recovered the *Nora*, the captain sent for me. He had drawn up an account of the incident, to be inserted in the ship's log and to be sent to the owners. He wanted me to look at it for corrections or amplifications. I made one suggestion and he adopted it. Then he said, "I have some further remarks that are not properly entries for the log. I'll send them on to the owners because they are of some importance. I would like you to know the tenor of those observations." And he handed me a sheet of paper.

The captain had written that in his opinion the survival of the *Nora Mason* was due first to the fact that a defective bomb had exploded in a relatively large space—if confined it might have generated much more destructive force, blowing up the munitions in the tweendecks and those in the lower hold. The second accident was the rupture of a pipe carrying live steam under pressure. That damage had stopped the ship's engines, but it also smothered the fire kindled by the explosion. A bomb that had been charged and armed correctly would have destroyed the ship at once; the troops and the crew would have been annihilated. He hoped that the owners would protest again the Army's ukase, and remind those responsible for this near-calamity that the United States was not a totalitarian nation, and its servants in the armed forces might not willfully endanger the lives and the goods of the sovereign people. He went on to say that the *Nora* was manned on this cruise by a capital crew. That was why the evacuation of the soldiers had been accomplished in minutes and without confusion or injuries. Then I read that the captain wanted to make particular mention of the conduct of the *Nora*'s first officer. He was young in years but nevertheless a thorough seaman. "On this occasion he had shown himself a steady and reliable officer, as indeed he had proved to be all during this extended cruise. Of course he has done no more than his duty, but he performed it at all times to my entire satisfaction. I have had occasion to speak about him with Captain Stone and Captain Connelly, under whom he has served, and I learned that they were very much of my mind. He holds the master's certificate. Since in the past you have been so good as to consult me about promotions, I take the liberty of proposing a candidate. I strongly recommend that the company appoint the first officer of the *Nora Mason* to a command when a berth falls vacant."

I was telling Diana how I had come to read those paragraphs, and I would have gone on to say how surprised I was by the codicil. When I began to thank him for his good opinion he cut me short. "I can tell you—in strict confidence—that there is a berth empty or shall be very shortly. I have been in correspondence with the man himself. He is retiring because of poor health." I would have gone on to tell her that, but I must have felt something. I turned to look at her. At first I could not see what was happening. Dredging up memories of a distant time puts you in another world, abstracted and dreamlike. Then I saw that she was crying. I was shocked that for a long while I had been reciting those recollections and not attending to what she might be feeling, reduced as she was by physical weakness and the moral flaw of a Cassandra. "Darling, what's the matter?" She said, "You were only a boy, and you had to act like a man."

The first thing that occurred to me was that the Procedure had left her with the gift that senses the tears of things. I was not myself conscious that there was anything to mourn in those faded memories. At the time the adventures came to me I did not think of myself as a tender youth who was forced to play the man. All my activity was simply doing the next thing. But the fact is that she saw beyond what I could see. Captain Nielsen had seen beyond the face that the Army presented from far places. He could not know positively what was being prepared for the *Nora;* his forebodings came to him nonetheless from halfway round the world. Halfway round the world and long years later

Diana wept not for that youngster but for the blind purposes of men. And the fact is that I have lived my life as a somnambulist. I am surprised now that for years I stared at the sun through a dark glass to find its height at noon. And that at morning and evening twilight I pointed the sextant at the bright navigational stars, and traced by them the lines of position with which we found our way upon the sea. Undeniably I had learned a clever trick. But what was it for? You embrace a profession and you learn a clever trick. There is a poem on this subject from the Spanish of my shipmate Juan Soto. It is called in English "Deep Song," after the *cante hondo* of the flamenco. It bears an epigraph, the first line of one such song, "*Quisiera yo renegar este mundo por entero*" — "I would renounce this world, utterly."

Well, we pulled out of Cadiz, we struck the long swell,
that fool skipper taking the seas abeam
as if he meant to roll the sticks out of her
or maybe shift the case goods in her hold.
I said, fine. Here goes Juan Soto. Why not? The deep song
says
I would renounce this world, oh utterly. This world —
two gulps of salt will cancel out this world, oh utterly.
Let her go. Let the company collect on the insurance.

But the shrouds held, the dunnage held the case goods
and the deck load. I'm still afloat,
still hauling some man's cargo on the ocean.
Hauling Juan Soto, a man I never liked, never trusted.

That is not a happy mood, surely. The plenitude of life eludes us. Only a trick of fancy gives us light and air. The overture of Bach's Orchestral Suite No. 1 in C Major opens up your chest with its candid surgery, beautiful and not happy—*la gaia scienza* is not happy—arguing the limits of life, and the consolations, which are mostly stoic. Educated in armies and navies like half the world, I was assured of certain certainties—all false. I have gone through life a somnambulist. The great Lope made drama of that condition, calling his play *La vida es sueño*, life is a dream. A dream of violence more often than not. And having proved his point, at the very end he asserts—of us—"All these are dreams, all dreams."